NORTHERN PASSAGES

Feisty tales of
"Growing Up North"

by Jerry Harju

NORTHERN PASSAGES

Feisty tales of
"Growing Up North"

by Jerry Harju

Illustrations by
Rick Humphrey

Copyright 1995
by Jerry Harju

Published by North Harbor Publishing
528 E. Arch St. Marquette, Michigan 49855
Toll Free (877) 906-3984
e-mail: jharju@bresnanlink.net

Publishing Coordination by
Globe Printing Inc. Ishpeming, Michigan

ISBN 0-9670205-3-0
Library of Congress Card No. 95-079065

First Edition - October 1995
Reprinted 1997, 2000

Introduction

This is the third book about my early years in Michigan's Upper Peninsula, and as you can see from the cover, I'm now getting into the sleazy, adult material. Just kidding—I *did* veer toward some sleaze in one of the stories, but this book, like the first two, is chock-full of wholesome adventures during my clean-cut boyhood. Admittedly, there *is* a nude scene in one of the stories, but it's well-hidden and you'll have to find it yourself.

I keep claiming that these stories are fictionalized, the names changed to protect the guilty, but some people in Marquette County think they recognize themselves and have sworn to get me. The beard and mustache that you see in my picture at the back of the book is one of the many disguises I use when skulking around Upper Michigan gathering story material.

It's been over four years since I began writing short stories, and I'd like to say a few words about writing.

Do I consider myself a writer? Not really—at least not yet. *Rewriter* is a more accurate description. Fully seventy-five percent of my writing time has been spent on rewriting. Practically every sentence in this book has been restructured, reworded, repunctuated, shortened, smoothed, and moved. In fact, I've rewritten this introduction eleven times.

I've learned more about the English language in the last four years than I have in the preceding fifty-eight. For example, do you know that there are about one hundred and fifty-four rules regarding hyphenated words? Pat Green, my sweetheart and chief editor, has memorized all of them and doesn't hesitate to drive them home with her little red pen. Her lectures on verb conjugation, compound sentences, dependent clauses, and misplaced phrases induce frightening flashbacks of sophomore-class sentence-diagramming in Republic High School in 1949.

And as if that isn't enough, my cousin Karen, a high-ranking officer in the Good-Taste Police, also attacks my material to keep it from becoming too repulsive. I *did*, however, fight back in defense of one of my stories. She claimed that little girls never pick their noses—I disagreed.

In conclusion, conjuring up story lines is relatively easy—getting them into polished prose is backbreaking work.

So why do I do it? For one thing, there has been nothing in my thirty-five-year aerospace engineering career as rewarding as writing these books of short stories.

The books are also part of my legacy. Long after I'm gone, anyone can pick up one of my books and get a chuckle or two (I hope). The book itself may become tattered and faded with age, but the prose will still be as fresh as the day I finished writing (rewriting) it. It's better than money—it doesn't depreciate, and it can't be misspent.

I always enjoy hearing from my readers. Drop me a line and say hello. Give me your opinion of the book—no matter what it is.

Jerry Harju
528 E. Arch St.
Marquette, MI 49855
Toll Free (877) 906-3984
e-mail: jharju@bresnanlink.net

Dedication

To Jeff (a.k.a. Kippy) Jacobs,
my partner in kid crimes
and
a lifelong friend.

Acknowledgements

Several people made valuable contributions to this book. I thank my sweetheart, best friend, and editor, Pat Green, who has been so instrumental in making this book a polished product and has become a grammar expert in the process of laboring long and hard over the text. I thank Rick Humphrey, whose delightful drawings have given the book a sparkling touch. I thank my cousin, Karen Murr, an experienced word mechanic who did a ring and valve job on many of my nouns, verbs, adjectives, and adverbs. Finally, I thank Cam, Chris, Eino, Harriet, Jeff, Jim, Kim, Margaret, Mike, Monteal, Roger, and others who reviewed the manuscript rough drafts.

Books by Jerry Harju

Northern Reflections
Northern D'lights
Northern Passages
The Class of '57
Cold Cash

Table of Contents

The Kindergarten Chronicles

*W*huddaya gotta do there?" I asked.

"Lotsa stuff," Kippy said. "One thing . . . you learn to pee fast."

"Huh?"

"You learn to pee fast . . . if ya don' finish peein' inna coupl'a minutes, the teacher comes in an' gets ya."

"Comes in where?"

"The bathroom. Sum kids, she hadda come in an' get 'em alla time."

"The *bathroom*? They make ya take *baths*?" This was going to be a lot worse than I had expected.

"Nah," Kippy said. "It's jus' toilets. I dunno why they call it a bathroom."

Kippy Jacobs and I were playing with our ragtag assortment of cast-iron toy cars and trucks in my backyard sandpile on South Second Street in Ishpeming, Michigan. September 1938—in a matter of days I was going to be subjected to an ordeal of unimaginable magnitude—kindergarten. Six-year-old Kippy was a year up on me and already a crafty one-year veteran of the school system. I was grilling him, figuring that any advance knowledge about the typical school day couldn't hurt.

"Whut if ya gotta poop? Ya only getta coupl'a minutes fer that, too?"

"You better do that at home," Kippy said wisely.

"But my ma sez they keep ya there till three o'clock." This was serious—my poops had no set schedule. "Wud else d'ya do?"

"Well . . . you sing."

"*Sing*? I dunno how t'sing."

"Teacher don' care . . . ya sing anyhow."

"How kin she make ya sing if ya don' know how?" Maybe it was like that John Dillinger movie—one of the two movies I had seen in my life—where the cops made the crook sing. This wasn't looking good. "Wud else?" I asked, not sure I wanted to hear more.

"You draw pichurrs."

This was the first good thing I'd heard. I had lots of experience drawing pictures on the butcher paper that our meat came wrapped in. Butcher paper was excellent for drawing, although you had to wipe off all the blood first.

"'Nother thing," Kippy added. "Ya gotta take a nap at two o'clock, so yer wide awake when it's time t'go home."

"I ain't sleepy at two o'clock."

"Ya gotta take a nap anyway."

Kippy continued with a chuckle, warming up to making me squirm. "Half the kids're girls, an' ya gotta sit next to 'em."

"I don' wanna go," I wailed.

Kippy smiled deviously, "You ought'a do wud I did."

"Whazzat?"

"Tell yer ma yer sick. I skipped th'first three days a kinnergarden cuz I tol' 'er I hadda bellyache."

That sounded like good advice.

Tuesday morning following Labor Day—zero hour—the first day of kindergarten.

"Ma, I don' feel s'good . . . I think I got th'chicken pox again."

My mother was dragging the comb through the sludge of Wildroot Creme Oil that she'd dumped on my hair. She paused just long enough to slap a hand on my forehead and command, "Stick out your tongue." Upon completing my ten-second physical examination, she lost all interest in my plight and resumed combing.

"I think I see sum red spots on my hand."

"You don't get chicken pox twice. You're going to school, and that's final." She had as much bedside manner as a railroad spike.

"But what if th'other kids catch sumthin' from me."

"You'll be catching something from *me* if you don't shut up."

Ten minutes later we trudged up to the school, my mother with an iron grip on my wrist. Kids and mothers converged on the building from every direction—pleading, yelling, and gnashing teeth—but that was the mothers, the kids were much too scared to make any noise. Panic-stricken, I craned my neck around, taking one last look at freedom—at the things I had so casually taken for granted all these years: sunshine, blue sky, and green grass.

Scritch—scritch—scritch—my corduroy knickers scraping together at the legs broadcasted my arrival for miles around. The knickers—part of my new-clothes-for-school package—were, like everything else I was wearing, stiff and itchy. Months before, my mother had measured every conceivable dimension of my body and shipped the information off to Sears, Roebuck & Co.

We melted into the throng entering the school. Grimly clutching a paper bag containing my box of Crayolas and a small pair of blunt-tipped scissors, I was ready for anything. Unescorted first-, second-, and third-graders pointed and sneered at the raw kindergarten recruits being dragged down the hallway in their mothers' grasp.

"Leggo my hand," I said. "I kin walk by myself."

"And have you make a break for it?" she snapped. "I'll let you loose when we get into the room."

The kindergarten room was huge—walls festooned with primitive drawings, agonizingly scratched out by previous inmates. Toward the rear of the room, little chairs were arranged in a neat circle. One wall held a large picture of two knock-'em-dead-good-looking kids and an oddly marked dog wearing a stupid grin on his muzzle. I would learn later that this was the famed Dick and Jane, and their dog Spot.

But the absolutely outstanding feature of the room was the pond—a real pond with real water—with *sailboats*.

Whenever a heavy rain puddled up my backyard, Kippy and I held fierce naval engagements. Our battleships were wooden clothespins. To have a pond inside a room with real honest-to-God model sailboats was the height of luxury.

I made a beeline for the pond, but of course, all the other boys had the same idea, and there was already a huge crowd around the edge.

The problem was quickly resolved by a big fat kid. He rumbled over, peeled away several of the kids who were hanging over the edge of the pond, and assumed command of the whole sailboat fleet in a matter of seconds. The rest of us scurried to safety. I had encountered my fair share of bullies on South Second Street and knew the consequences of not moving out of range fast enough.

My mother took care of registration, gave me a quick hug, and whispered assorted threats into my ear about what would happen if I didn't behave in class. As the mothers departed, a wave of anxiety swept through the room. Anticipating this, the teacher hurriedly closed the door, herded us over to the circle of chairs, and began talking before the realization set in that we were now flying solo.

"Hello, girls and boys. My name is Miss Henshaw; I'm your kindergarten teacher . . . " She droned on at some length about how much fun we were going to have and that we were all going to become very good friends. I didn't believe that for one second—half the class were girls.

"The first thing we'll do this morning is to learn how to sing a song. How many of you know how to sing a song?" Only a few hands went up. Miss Henshaw beamed confidently. "That's okay, children, I'll teach you how; the name of this song is 'Old McDonald.'"

"Old McDonald" started off with his duck—with a quack-quack here and a quack-quack there. The girl sitting next to me thought that was the most wonderful thing she had ever heard, and even when we moved on to the pig, with an oink-oink here and an oink-oink there—which I considered far superior to the duck—she just kept on quacking away.

We labored along through the turkey, goose, cow, and chicken. Each kid had picked a key of his choice, and as the song gained momentum, the room pulsed with screechy, hysterical cackles, gobbles, cheeps, peeps, yowls, growls, honks, and moos. My head was throbbing. The girl next to me quacked through the entire menagerie like a stuck phonograph record. Just as I was seriously considering bopping the duck-girl on top of the head to jar her loose, Miss Henshaw exhausted her repertoire of barnyard animals and the song ground mercifully to a halt. I'll bet Old McDonald would have sold the whole lot to a butcher shop to get some peace and quiet.

Next, a snack break featuring cupcakes and milk replenished the energy burned up on "Old McDonald." I loved cupcakes—maybe this kindergarten business wasn't so bad after all.

Another woman walked into the room. "This is Miss Cox," Miss Henshaw said. "She's going to help us go to the bathroom. I'll take the boys, and Miss Cox will take the girls."

The milk curdled in my stomach. This is what Kippy warned me about—the dreaded *bathroom*. They divided us up by sex and marched us down the hallway in two separate lines. The girl's line swerved off and headed through a door, while the boys kept going down to the far corner.

"This is the boys' bathroom," Miss Henshaw said in a business-like tone. "Go in and go to the bathroom, but don't dawdle, or I'll have to come in and get you."

What does she mean . . . go in and go to the bathroom?
I thought this WAS the bathroom. What's dawdle? Is that like
peeing? Isn't that what we're supposed to do?

But no one had enough nerve to question the instructions—we all scurried through the door, intent on completing our mission.

Sure enough, there was a toilet in there—surrounded by metal walls with a metal door hanging open. The big fat kid who had commandeered the sailboats dashed over to it. He grinned triumphantly at us through the open stall door, dropped his pants, and sat down. *He was going to poop.* This was bad news. A kid his size would probably take a long poop. The rest of us stood around waiting, nervously shifting from one foot to the other.

There were four little sinks on one wall and four odd-looking things mounted on the opposite wall—made out of the same stuff as toilets, but they weren't toilets.

A much bigger kid—probably a third-grader—swaggered in. He bellied up to one of those things and showed us what they were for. With sighs of relief, several kids followed suit; however, precious time had been lost. There were still about a dozen of us waiting, and Miss Henshaw was due in at any moment.

At last it was my turn, but my bladder was paralyzed with anxiety. I just stood there, praying for a dribble—a drop—anything. Nothing. Finally, I zipped up, nonchalantly turned around with a smile of satisfaction, and pretended that everything had gone according to plan.

It could have been much worse—at least I had a zipper on my pants. One kid had about thirty-eight buttons, and by the time the rest of us were going out the door, he had just gotten unbuttoned.

5

We lined up in the hallway, and Miss Henshaw, counting heads, realized she was missing one. Without a word, she barged into the boys' bathroom and, moments later, emerged with the button-kid in tow. We marched back to the kindergarten room, while he furiously buttoned up on the way.

Paper chains were next on our busy agenda. We all sat on the floor, and Miss Henshaw passed around strips of colored paper and library paste. She demonstrated how the chains were made—making a loop with the paper strip, pasting the ends together to form a circle, and then attaching each new strip as another link.

I was no stranger to paste, having mixed my own at home on many occasions, using flour and water. The best way to tell if you had a good batch was to taste it, so I stuck a finger in the library paste and took a nip just to see if they had mixed it correctly. It sure didn't taste like the stuff I made at home—wasn't bad, though, and I tried a second fingerful. A couple of other kids spotted me, thought it was worth a try, and dipped into their paste.

"Don't eat the library paste," Miss Henshaw shrilled. This tempted others to sample the stuff, starting a riot of paste eating. It was several minutes before Miss Henshaw restored order.

Making paper chains was no big deal; in no time at all I had a dandy with six links of different colors. But the big fat kid couldn't seem to grasp the concept. He was making paper loops but not linking them together. That was probably why he was so big: he had been here for years wrestling with the logic of making paper chains.

It was time to go to the bathroom again and none too soon to suit me. My bladder, having passed up the earlier opportunity, was now complaining bitterly and threatening to mutiny at any minute. The button-kid, a fast learner, jockeyed into a strategic position at the head of the line and started unbuttoning his pants as we went down the hall, thereby denying Miss Henshaw a chance to yank him out of the bathroom again. I got to be an old hand at using the wall thingamajig, even discovering a lever for flushing.

Lunch was a big disappointment—peanut butter and jelly sandwiches, milk, and apples—no cupcakes. Miss Henshaw reassembled us for the strenuous afternoon session. "All right, children, this afternoon we're going to draw a picture. How many of you have drawn a picture before?" Several hands shot up, mine being one. When it came to drawing, I was a virtuoso.

Miss Henshaw chirped on. "We're going to draw a ball. I'll pass out paper and crayons, and we'll see who can draw the best ball."

A ball? That's it? I'll win for sure!

A ball was nothing compared to some of my creations on butcher paper. Just the week before, I had drawn an excellent likeness of the iron-ore train that chugged past our house every hour. I *did* have to explain to my mother what it was, but then she never had much appreciation for fine art.

Miss Henshaw passed out two pieces of paper to each kid—in case you had to start over—and three crayons: red, yellow, and black. You got to pick what color to make your ball, but how could you possibly design a prize-winning ball with only red, yellow, and black to choose from? I chuckled to myself as I reached into my paper bag from home and withdrew my forty-eight-color set of Crayolas—the Cadillac of crayon sets.

I deliberated over my color selection. I'd yet to read my first book, but I had badgered my mother into teaching me to read the names of the forty-eight colors in the set. Ignoring the more mundane colors, I went directly to my favorites—burnt sienna, turquoise, apricot, magenta, salmon, and Prussian blue.

I made my decision. "I think I'll make a turquoise ball," I confided to the kid kneeling on the floor next to me, gnawing pensively on his black crayon. He gave me a blank stare.

I quickly found that drawing a ball was a bigger job than I realized—I couldn't draw a round circle. My first try looked more like a hippopotamus. Then, spotting the round Tinkertoy can sitting on the floor with other toys, I sidled over, picked up the can, and put it on my second piece of paper. Taking my turquoise crayon, I traced around the bottom of the can. Aha—a perfect circle. Humming to myself, I colored it in and in a matter of minutes, I had the ball done.

The kid next to me was having an awful time. His black ball resembled a giant, half-chewed raisin. Feeling charitable since I was certain to take top honors with my turquoise ball, I decided to help him out.

"There's a better way to make a ball," I told him.

"Huh?"

"Here . . . lemme show ya." I placed the Tinkertoy can on his spare piece of paper. He looked at it, dumbstruck.

"Take yer crayon an' run it around th'bottom of th'can," I explained.

He did, saw the results, and gaped at me like I had invented the electric light bulb. We just stared at each other. At that moment we both knew he owed me one. "My name's Jimmy," he said.

Miss Henshaw walked around and looked at everybody's ball, giving each kid a generous helping of oooh's and aaah's. Jimmy's ball got special praise. "What a nice ball, James . . . so *round!*" He smiled modestly. Then she looked at mine, hesitated, but only murmured, "Very nice."

"Well, girls and boys, the balls are all so good that I can't decide whose ball is the best . . . "

Can't decide whose ball is the best? I stared at my ball in disbelief. *What was wrong with it? She didn't like the color—that was it—she only gave us red, yellow, and black crayons and got mad because I used turquoise.*

"We'll just say that they're all winners. Be sure to take your drawing home and show it to your mommy and daddy . . . "

It was obvious—the school system didn't appreciate independent thinkers.

"Time to wake up, children . . . "

Miss Henshaw's syrupy voice broke through the cobwebs in my brain. We had been taking the compulsory two-o'clock nap on pallets on the kindergarten floor—I had been in the midst of a nightmare involving wearing a pair of corduroy knickers with two hundred buttons on the fly.

"In the time remaining, you may play with the dolls, the Tinkertoys, the sailboats . . . "

The sailboats! I was instantly wide awake. All day I had been looking wistfully at the sailboats, wondering if we were ever going to get a chance at them. My pallet was close to the pond, so I jumped up and easily beat out the herd of boys who charged over.

I had just grabbed the best boat—a sleek, white job with red sails—when my hair stood on end, mainly because somebody behind me was pulling it straight up. My head jerked back violently, and I was flipped over on my back.

"Tha's *my* boat, ya dumb cluck." The big fat kid leaned over and threateningly pushed his face into mine. Peanut butter fumes drifted into my nose.

But Miss Henshaw had seen the assault. "Stop it, Roland. Everybody has a right to play with the sailboats." She shook a scolding finger at him, but that was all—she then turned her attention to two girls wanting to learn the intricacies of jumping rope. I couldn't believe she hadn't clobbered him. My mother would have raised a baseball-sized knot on his head if she had been in charge of this operation.

Roland scowled and backed off for awhile, but as soon as the coast was clear, he shoved kids away from the pond, gathering up as many of the best boats as he could. He then leaned over the pond with his ample hindquarters sticking up in the air and displayed his total ignorance of things nautical by going "chug-chug-chug" as he pushed a sailboat around the water.

I started to walk away—there was nothing else to do. Maybe the Lone Ranger, the Green Hornet, or the Shadow could deal out swift justice to over-sized bad guys, but in real life, the thugs I ran across in South Ishpeming got their way day in and day out. Why should this time be different?

But this time *was* different. Out of nowhere, with superhero speed, an avenging force rushed by me—doing what every red-blooded boy in the room had been aching to do—booting Roland right in the center of his big butt. A beautiful kick—the avenger burying his foot up to the ankle in fanny fat. Roland lifted out over the water and hung there for a split second. Then he hit.

SSSPPPLLLOOOOUUUUSSSHHH!!!!

Every cubic inch of water in the shallow pond squirted up and out of the way to make room for Roland, drenching kids within a radius of ten feet. The sailboat fleet was in instant dry dock.

9

Doing what every red-blooded boy in the room had been aching to do—booting Roland right in the center of his big butt.

I found myself cheering and clapping my hands. Jimmy, the kicker, bounded over to me with triumphant glee and threw an arm across my shoulder. "Whaddaya think a that, ol' pal?"

Miss Henshaw snapped her head around as soon as she heard the commotion. She saw Jimmy and me standing behind Roland's prone body, Jimmy with his arm around me, and both of us grinning like a couple of Cheshire cats. "James! Gerald! What have you two done?"

The smile dropped off my face—wait a minute—did she say, "What have you *two* done?"

Roland lay in the bottom of the pool, his clothes quickly blotting up the remainder of the water. He was screaming his head off.

"WHAAAAAAARRRRRGGGGGGGGGHHHHHHHHH!!!!!!"

Miss Henshaw rushed over and lifted him out of the pond—no small job since he now weighed a ton with all the water. After making sure he was all right, she marched over to Jimmy and me. "You two go over and stand in the corner," she snapped. "I'm keeping you after school."

I looked at Jimmy with alarm as we walked hurriedly to the corner. "Whazzat that mean . . . keeping you after school?"

I think it means we can't go home at three o'clock. We're bein' punished."

"I didn' do nuthin'! *Yer* th'one that kicked th'fat kid."

"Yeah, but I did it 'cause he shoved ya, an' yer my pal."

"I don' even *know* ya," I cried.

"Sure ya do . . . you showed me how t'make a ball, 'member?"

"But that don' make us pals."

Jimmy's eyes narrowed suspiciously. "Don' ya wanna be my pal?"

"Well . . . yeah . . . sure I do."

"You ain' a pal a th'fat kid, are ya?"

"I hate 'im . . . but she thinks I helped ya kick 'im in th'pond."

"So? Pals gotta stick together . . . they don' squeal on each other," Jimmy stated with finality.

I was trapped—no avenue of escape—I had to take the rap with Jimmy. He had evoked the unwritten law of the backyards and alleys of

Ishpeming: pals don't squeal on each other. "How long you think she's gonna keep us after school? My ma's cummin t'get me at three o'clock."

Jimmy cast an appraising eye on the mass disruption he had generated. Kids were crying, running around out of control. Miss Henshaw had brought in Miss Cox to help sop up the water and wring out the kids who had been too close to the pond.

"I dunno . . . mebbe she'll call th'police," Jimmy speculated.

"Th'police? They gonna put us in jail?" I squeaked.

Jimmy grinned with anticipation. "Always wanted to see th'jail."

I edged away. This kid was beyond weird. "I don' wanna go t'jail. I gotta go home fer supper."

"They'll give ya supper in jail."

"Whut do they give ya?" Not cupcakes, I thought. Probably warmed-over hash—we had a lot of that at home.

"Moldy bread an' water," Jimmy said.

"Whut about dessert?" I asked.

"The *first* day? THE VERY *FIRST* DAY?" my mother yelled. "Thirteen years of school ahead of you, and you get into trouble the *first* day?"

My mother, Miss Henshaw, and I were standing—or more accurately, they were standing and I was cringing—at Miss Henshaw's desk. It was three-fifteen, and the other kids had gone home—after the mothers of the soggy ones had glared at Jimmy and me standing in the corner.

Jimmy had gotten a very speedy trial. After hearing the charges, his mother just grabbed him by the ear and hauled him out. He got off easy compared to what I was in for. My mother had a penchant for pulling my hair straight up until I was on my tiptoes. The school was only a short four-block walk from our house, but it would seem a lot longer doing it on tiptoes.

"Don't be too hard on Gerald," Miss Henshaw said to my mother. "The other boy confessed to me that he was the one who actually kicked Roland into the pond." She lowered her voice. "And in fact, Roland was asking for it. Your son was only cheering James on."

Smiling at me, she added, "Why don't you show your mother the ball you drew?" I handed the drawing of the turquoise ball to my mother, fully expecting that in her present state of mind she would probably rip it up and feed me the pieces.

"It was the best drawing in the whole class," Miss Henshaw confided.

I looked at her in disbelief. *"The whole class?"*

"It was so good that it might have discouraged the rest of the children if I had showed it to them. It's a beautiful ball. Where did you get the blue crayon?"

"Turquoise," I said.

"What?"

"It's turquoise." I pulled out the crayon box and pointed to the label on the turquoise crayon.

"You can *read?*"

"Only the crayons," my mother said modestly. "I taught him to read the colors on all his crayons."

"Amazing," Miss Henshaw said. "He's going to be a very good student, I'm sure."

"Maybe . . . if he quits hanging around with troublemakers." My mother said in a calmer tone of voice. She took a long look at the turquoise ball. "The best one . . . ," she murmured, shaking her head, trying to recall if anyone in our family had ever been the best at anything. She gave me back the drawing and took my hand. "C'mon, let's go home. I have to get started on supper."

The turquoise ball had saved my life. As we walked down the sidewalk from the school, I made a mental note to immediately start on a portfolio of drawings. You never know when you might need something like that to get out of a tight spot. I sucked in the fresh air, amazed and grateful to be free.

Standing at the curb, gabbing about the rigors of the first day of school, were two mothers with their kids from my kindergarten class. One of them was the duck-girl. She spotted me and with an idiotic smile started up with a flirtatious, "Quack-quack-quack-quack . . . "

I gently disengaged my hand from my mother's, threw back my shoulders, and looked straight ahead as we passed. A student of my caliber had to show *some* dignity.

It had been a long hectic day. The kindergarten experience had aged me—I felt like I was at least eight. But it had been exciting, and I was anxious to tell my mother of all the new things I had seen and done.

"Ma, they got a room with four funny-looking little thingamajigs hanging on the wall that you pee into . . . "

"Don't start telling me fibs," she snapped. "Haven't you been in *enough* trouble for one day?"

The Witch's Picnic

The room was hushed. I aligned my body perfectly on the center of the piano bench, flexed my fingers, and poised them over the keys of the beginning E minor chord. I locked my eyes on the sheet music of "The Song of the Volga Boatmen" and began to play. I got through the first chord transition to the A minor chord successfully, but moments later, my fingers struck a totally random assortment of keys. The piano vibrated with a harsh, grating sound—the Volga boatmen had run aground.

Teddy, my trusty dog, was snoozing by the living room stove, paws twitching as he chased rabbits through his dream. The discordant notes woke him with a start, and he quickly scrambled to his feet, whirling around to see what the noise was. When he spotted me at the piano, he lay back down with his head between his paws, muttered a couple of doggy curses, and closed his eyes.

I'd always thought that a piano player just flopped down at a piano, looked at the keys, and started playing. However, Miss Louella Wigg—the renowned music virtuoso and piano teacher of Ishpeming, Michigan—set me straight. There were strict rules for piano playing. The worst of these was the no-looking-at-the-keys rule. You kept your eyes firmly fixed on the sheet music—like flying an airplane by instruments.

At age seven, this idea was so inconceivable to me that I ignored it for the first three months of my lessons. So my piano playing went something like this: look at the sheet music, then down at the keyboard to find the right keys, press the keys, look back up at the music, back down at the keyboard, press the keys, and so on. At that rate "The Minute Waltz" would take nineteen years. Miss Wigg finally laid down the law about that, so on a wintery Saturday afternoon in December 1940, I sat at the scarred upright piano in our living room, determined to master the no-looking-at-the-keys rule.

Eyes glued to the sheet music, I relentlessly worked on the opening measure, totally mangling the music every time. I looked at the Regulator clock on the kitchen wall. Twenty more minutes and my mandatory half-hour of torture would be over.

I never dreamed that anything could be worse than a Saturday-night sauna, but piano lessons took the honors. My mother, however, had made it quite clear that it wasn't a topic for debate. Esther, my seventeen-year-old sister, had been playing piano for many years, but next year she was leaving for college. With my mother hopelessly hooked on command-performance piano concerts in our living room, I had been selected as the heir-apparent house-piano-player.

My old man was sitting in his wooden rocking chair with his daily newspaper, *The Mining Journal*, hoping to make some sense out of the war in Europe, and each time I sank the Volga boatmen, his knuckles tightened up another notch on the newspaper.

"What's that yer playin'?" he finally asked.

"It's a Russian boat song."

"Sounds more like a Nazi tank attack," he replied.

My fingers slammed into a particularly hideous chord, and Teddy got up, slunk out to the kitchen, and scratched on the back door.

My mother was peeling potatoes at the kitchen table. "What's wrong with that dog? It's ten below zero out there, and he wants to go out again. I just let him out an hour ago."

"Nuthin' wrong with 'im," the old man replied. "He's just a music critic."

Forced smiles of encouragement were putting a tremendous strain on Miss Wigg's thick layer of makeup the following Monday during my piano lesson. Cracks appeared around the corners of her mouth.

"Don't look at your hands, Gerald; keep your eyes on the music." She had a high, quavery voice, like a loon in mating season. Her parlor clock chimed the hour, and with a sigh of relief I started to slide off the piano bench. She held up her hand. "We're not quite finished. I have a special

surprise . . . something that will give you an incentive to practice harder."
She smiled again, dislodging a fragment of makeup that rolled off her jaw
and onto her lap.

"What kinda surprise?" I asked suspiciously. Teachers never handed
out good surprises.

"I'm going to put on a recital."

"What's a recital?"

"All my students will participate in a piano concert at the Methodist
Church. You'll be able to demonstrate your piano-playing skills for the public. Won't that be nice?"

"Y'mean I'm gonna play the piano in church in front of a whole
bunch a people?"

"That's right."

"Do I hafta?"

Her pleasant expression wilted. "Of course you do . . . all my students will be taking part."

"But I still make lots'a mistakes. Nobody's gonna like it."

"I expect you to practice hard for this recital, but in the event you
make a mistake or two, I've chosen a piece where it won't be noticeable."
She produced several sheets of music and put them up on the piano. "This
is what you'll be playing."

"'The Fairy's Picnic?' Did a Russian write this one, too?"

"No. I composed it myself," she purred modestly.

I thumbed through the music. "I gotta play this whole thing? It's
pretty long."

"If you'll look closely at the tablature, you'll notice that it has three
parts . . . you'll only be playing one-third of the music you see there."

"Three parts?"

"Three students will be playing it. You'll be one of them."

"Do we take turns?"

"You'll be all playing at the same time. It will be very pretty."

"On one piano?"

"Yes. Since you're all children, you'll fit nicely side by side on the
piano bench. And you needn't worry . . . the other two students are more
advanced and will be playing the difficult parts. If you make a mistake, it
probably won't be heard."

"Who are the other two kids?" I asked.

"Carlotta LaRoc and Iris Baumgarten."
"I'm gonna hafta play the piano with *two girls?*"

I slogged morosely through the gray winter slush on the way home, my mind frantically groping for a way out of the recital. By the time I reached the house I had concocted a sure-fire scheme.

My mother was jamming the last of Sunday's roast beef into the meat grinder for the week's supply of hash, and the old man was hunched over the kitchen table pouring steaming coffee from his cup into the saucer to cool it down.

"Ma," I said in a nonchalant tone. "Ya know that new washing machine you want? I know how you kin get some money t'pay for it."

She started to grind up the beef. "Oh? What's that?"

"We sell the piano."

My mother didn't even look up. "You're going to keep taking piano lessons, and that's final."

I switched to my backup plan—whining for mercy. "But Miss Wigg's gonna make me play in a recital, an' it's gonna sound awful. Please tell her I can't do it."

That got her attention. "A recital? When?"

"January 12, in the Methodist Church."

"Why, that's wonderful. We'll tell all the relatives and neighbors. What are you going to play?"

"'The Fairy's Picnic' . . . somethin' Miss Wigg wrote herself . . . but that's not the worst part. I'm gonna hafta play it with two girls."

"Who are they?"

"Carlotta LaRoc and Big Bum Baumgarten."

"Don't talk like that . . . call her Iris."

The old man looked up. "Ain't that Clyde Baumgarten's girl? Y'know he manages the A&P store. Y'ought'a get t'know 'er." The old man reasoned that getting acquainted with someone whose father managed something as large as the A&P store was a step up the social ladder and an opportunity that shouldn't be passed up.

"Those girls are a little older than you, aren't they?" my mother asked.

"A little older? They're *old ladies*! Both of 'em are in the fifth grade."

She started to cut up the leftover boiled potatoes into the ground-up roast beef. "Well, I think it's really nice . . . you getting to play in a recital." She shot the old man a triumphant leer. "I told you he was smart enough to learn the piano."

The old man blew on his saucer of coffee and took a long slurp. "Never said he wasn't smart. He thought of sellin' the piano, didn't he?"

A week later, the kickoff meeting of "The Fairy's Picnic" piano players was held. Miss Wigg could hardly contain her eagerness as she herded us into her parlor, hovering and clucking in her high-pitched voice like a loon mother hen with three little chicks.

Two of the chicks weren't little by any stretch of the imagination. Iris came by her nickname of Big Bum legitimately, measuring, as my old man would delicately put it, three ax handles across the beam. A slow-moving girl with thick glasses, she had an extraordinary tangle of wire braces on her front teeth and two short braids of muddy-brown hair that stuck out at oblique angles from her head.

Carlotta held the honor of being the only girl in the elite South Ishpeming French and Italian gang. She had declared herself one of the gang after pounding up on half the members. Ten years old, she towered over me by a foot and a half. I always gave Carlotta a wide berth. One day last summer, Terry Thompson and I were squatting in the dirt on Second Street playing marbles when Carlotta walked by. Terry shot a furtive peek up her dress, and without even breaking stride, she drop-kicked him across the street.

Many a time, at a safe distance, I had also looked enviously at her solid, sinewy body, hoping that one day I might have a build like that.

Miss Wigg finger-fluttered us over to the sofa and began to explain the story line of "The Fairy's Picnic."

"This takes place in an enchanted forest. Three creatures will be there . . . a fairy invites a mischievous elf and a little bear to a picnic." She inhaled expectantly, smiling and pausing for our enthusiastic response. Iris gazed out the window and picked her nose. Carlotta idly peeled a scab off of one of her swollen knuckles.

"Each part on the piano . . . each one of you, that is . . . will be a musical representation of one of these creatures. All of you have had a week to practice one of the parts, and now I'll tell you which part you've been working on. Carlotta, you're the fairy . . . Iris, you're the little bear . . . and Gerald, you're the mischievous elf."

Iris sat bolt upright. "A bear? That's what I've been practicing all week? A bear?" Her face coiled up into a peevish pout. "I know why you want me to be the bear. Cause you think I'm fat . . . like a bear. Well, I don't wanna be the bear . . . I wanna be the fairy . . . let Carlotta be the bear." The words whistled angrily through her braces.

Carlotta looked at her with cold, ebony eyes. "You're gonna be fatter in a second cause I'm gonna give you a fat lip if you don't shaddup. If you think I'm gonna be a bear in front of a church full of people, you gotta 'nother think comin'."

Miss Wigg began to wring her lace handkerchief. "Girls . . . stop that! . . . Iris, it's not a big *fat* bear. It's a little *cuddly* bear . . . " She spent the next ten minutes trying to pacify Iris. Since my position as mischievous elf didn't appear to be in immediate jeopardy, I kept my mouth shut.

We gathered up the sheet music and trooped over to the piano for our first attempt at playing all three parts together. Miss Wigg seated me in the middle. With Iris to the left and Carlotta to the right, it was like sitting between two elephants in a pickup truck.

We couldn't make our way through three measures without one of us falling out of sync with the others, and at times, each of us were playing at totally different parts of the piece. Finally, Miss Wigg pulled out her metronome, a little mechanical thingamabob resembling a pendulum clock standing on its head. This was supposed to keep us synchronized with one another, but it didn't help much. One thing was clear. If "The Fairy's Picnic" was ever going to sound like anything, I was going to log in a lot of time snuggled in between Iris and Carlotta.

Piano-player boot camp began. Miss Wigg and my mother alternated as drill sergeants. In her quest for the perfect recital, Miss Wigg called for rehearsals any time she could get the fairy, the elf, and the bear together. My mother levied an extra half-hour of practice time at home everyday, as well.

Christmas came and went. My life was slipping away, and all I had to show for it was a collection of ugly bruises, courtesy of Iris and Carlotta who battered me in search of more room on the piano bench. Hour after hour was spent huddled between Iris and Carlotta—elbows and hands slashing down on both sides of me like giant pistons.

Much as I hated to admit it, "The Fairy's Picnic" was actually starting to shape up. If this recital turned out to be the success that Miss Wigg and my mother were hoping for, I would be shackled to that piano bench forever. Something had to be done—*fast.*

Then, in my darkest hour, Providence lit a tiny candle. It was such a little thing, really, that I almost missed it.

We were in Miss Wigg's parlor, playing "The Fairy's Picnic" for the seventeen-thousandth time, when I accidentally brushed Carlotta's left hand with my right—easy to do since we were only one piano key apart on some of the passages. Her deflected hand missed its assigned bright and happy C major chord and struck a murky C minor.

"Damn," she snarled under her breath, thinking she blew it. She recovered, and "The Fairy's Picnic" gamboled on its merry way, but the embryo of an ingenious plan was forming. I had to test it. Three measures later I casually flicked my left wrist, only an inch or so, brushing Iris's right hand out of position. "The Fairy's Picnic" lurched again. Iris gave me a quick glance but wasn't really sure what had happened.

Miss Wigg was sitting by the window, daydreaming of thunderous applause from the recital audience, when her trained ear heard the brief discord. She hurried over to the piano, listening and watching, but the moment had passed. The three of us were now gaily tripping through the enchanted forest in perfect harmony.

I ran all the way home in the gray twilight, eager to get to the piano, study the sheet music carefully, and of course, practice. My mind raced, nourishing the idea, embellishing, fleshing out the details. Like most big capers, it was risky—even physically dangerous, but the payoff was worth it. I'd get my life back.

During the week before the recital, I practically lived at the keyboard, pouring diligently over the sheet music of "The Fairy's Picnic," and practicing like I had never practiced before—every afternoon and evening. My mother was impressed. Some nights, she had to tell me to quit and go to bed. By now, I could play the mischievous elf flawlessly, without looking at my hands or even the sheet music. Even the old man looked up from his newspaper from time to time and listened.

The First Methodist Church was filled to capacity a half-hour before the recital. Good—the more people the better. "The Fairy's Picnic" was last on the program. Unlike the other pieces in the recital, it was Miss Wigg's own composition, and she wanted it to be the grand finale. It would be *the* grand finale all right, I thought.

Miss Wigg had come up with one of her characteristically elegant touches. She'd decided that it would be very nice if the three of us were dressed befitting our parts. Carlotta was told to dress in something white and lacy, like a fairy. Iris, as the bear, was to wear plain brown, although an argument could have been made that Michigan bears were black. Miss Wigg arbitrarily decided that elves dressed in green, so my mother fashioned a vest and a triangular hat from some leftover, green Christmas wrapping paper. I looked like a sawed-off Robin Hood, without bow and arrows.

All of the recital participants were herded into the front pews. Carlotta was dazzling in the white dress she had worn two years earlier as flower girl at her Aunt Emily's second wedding. Of course, she had grown some since that affair. Now the hem only reached mid thigh and the puffed sleeves were drum-tight around her bulging biceps.

Clyde Baumgarten had brought home a pair of brown-twill work pants and a shirt from his A&P store. His wife shortened the pant legs and sewed the bill from one of Clyde's old hunting caps to the seat to look like a bear's tail. She painstakingly cut the logo off the back of the shirt, but the material underneath hadn't faded with the rest of the shirt, so Iris looked like a bear who had been branded by the A&P Company. But these were trivial details. Miss Wigg was very pleased with the overall appearance of her star trio.

The recital began with Miss Wigg giving a short speech extolling the talent and hard work of her students. She assured the audience that even though we were in a church, it was okay to applaud after each selection.

Nancy Aho led off with a pleasant, if somewhat choppy, rendition of "Beautiful Ohio." Jimmy LaForge followed next with "The Skater's Waltz," although it sounded as if the skater fell on his butt a few times. Kid after kid trooped up to the piano—airing the compositions that had been slaved over these many weeks.

At the end of each piece, Miss Wigg looked to the audience expectantly, hoping for an enthusiastic response, but it was not a warm crowd. There was only scattered, polite applause after each number—people were just not comfortable clapping in church. Besides, most of the men—the pianists' fathers, uncles, and brothers—had been dragged there against their wishes by wives and mothers. Arvo Millimaki began to snore halfway through "The Bells of Saint Mary's." His wife elbowed him viciously in the ribs, producing a loud snort which wasn't on the downbeat. It threw Elsie Mattila's timing off entirely. It was safe to say that the recital wasn't going to be the highlight of Ishpeming's winter social season.

Finally, it was our turn. Miss Wigg got up and addressed the now-stupefied listeners.

"The last presentation of the evening is my own composition entitled 'The Fairy's Picnic.' Unique in that it's written for three parts on the piano, 'The Fairy's Picnic' is set in an enchanted forest . . . "

She bla-bla-ed on at some length about her brainchild before introducing Carlotta, Iris, and me. The three of us walked up from the front pew and took our assigned seating on the piano bench. My heart was pounding—Carnegie Hall would have to be a piece of cake compared to what I was about to do.

"The Fairy's Picnic" began with Carlotta doing a fancy high-range melody line—two octaves above middle C—with her right hand, as the fairy called out to the mischievous elf and the little bear to come and join her in a picnic. She added a counterpoint rhythm with the left hand, weaving in the full, rich texture of the fairy's bell-like voice. I fingered the elf's reply with my right hand but just at the proper moment, poked my little finger out a fraction, right over a key that I knew Carlotta was going to play. The timing was perfect, as it had to be. Her left little finger bounced off my right little finger, and the fairy stuttered badly.

At this point the little bear began to answer the invitation, growling a response to the fairy. Iris started pounding out a series of growly, little-bear-like chord progressions, but I invoked the same stratagem, this time using my left little finger. The little bear gagged on her little tongue.

I had just launched an extremely dangerous and devious scheme, but if I ever hoped to end my piano-playing career, I had to bring a plague of ants to "The Fairy's Picnic." It would have been a simple matter just to screw up the elf's part, but Miss Wigg had written me in only as a bit player in the piece. Carlotta and Iris dominated the score. So in order to get the job done, the elf had to bushwhack the fairy and the little bear. I was convinced that after my mother listened to this and overheard the muffled snickers from the audience, she'd *gladly* put the piano up for sale.

Miss Wigg had assigned me one task that was crucial to my plan. Since I was sitting in the middle of the bench, I had the job of turning the pages of the sheet music. As we staggered down the first page, I picked up the elf's tempo. Not much, just enough so that by the time I got down to the bottom of the page, Carlotta and Iris were half a measure behind me. I quickly flipped the page.

"Slow down, ya lil' turd," the fairy rasped under her breath. The little bear got confused and dropped a few notes to catch up.

Now we were at the part where the fairy, the elf, and the little bear were searching the enchanted forest for a place to have their picnic. The score depicted the trio strolling happily down an enchanted path, hand in hand. But with an evil grin, the elf sped ahead along the path, the fairy and the little bear in hot pursuit. The little bear stumbled badly, probably over an enchanted tree root. Naturally, the elf got to the bottom of the second page before the other two, and he reached up to turn the sheet. The fairy, now lagging behind by three full measures, smashed the sheet music down with her left hand to keep this from happening. The sound reverberated throughout the church, waking up several fathers.

Miss Wigg rushed to the piano, furiously winding her metronome in the hope of restoring order. However, it only added an exotic syncopation to the tempo, conveying the impression that a tribe of Amazon headhunters had joined the race through the enchanted forest.

On the third page, the elf sped up and slowed down at will, flicking out his mischievous little fingers to the right and left at critical junctures.

In desperation, the little bear decided that if she had more elbow room, there wouldn't be so many mistakes, so she moved over to the far left side of the piano bench. This shifted its center of gravity, and the other end of the bench started to rise precariously off the floor. The fairy wasn't any lightweight either, but to restore stability, she had to hike out over the far right side of the bench like the crew on a heeling sailboat.

The fairy was really angry now and started taking it out on the piano with savage, decisive strokes. No longer could the listener picture a lovely, gossamer-winged creature, clad in diaphanous, white vestments. Instead, the thunderous, sharp chords portrayed some monster fairy from the swamp, stomping down Main Street, devouring the townspeople. In fact, when the elf stuck out his little finger again to obstruct one of her F chords,

This shifted the center of gravity, and the other end of the bench started to rise precariously off the floor.

the fairy hammered the finger into the keys with her rock-hard fist. "Hah! Gotcha that time, ya lil' fart," she whispered fiercely.

No matter, I thought, as I turned over the next page of the sheet music with two of my remaining good fingers, secure in the knowledge that "The Fairy's Picnic" was beyond redemption.

Since unruly and rebellious momentum was building, I took my hands off the keyboard entirely, figuring that it was unsafe to expose my fingers unnecessarily. This was a wise move because the fairy, spying a hand out of the corner of her eye, smashed it into the keys out of sheer spite. The little bear yowled in pain.

The end was near, and I sat back to savor a job well done. For the first time, my ears tuned in to the total sound. On my left, Iris, the little bear, stumbled around the keyboard with one remaining good paw, some five measures behind. On my right was Carlotta, the monster fairy, slashing down on the keys, exterminating everything within reach. On top of the piano, completely ignored by everyone, was the metronome, busily tick-tocking away. My ear drums were assaulted by deafening, harsh, frenzied chords—the sounds fusing together with demonic energy. The score was weaving itself into a villainous tapestry—a life and death struggle between the little bear and the fairy—between innocence and evil. Emerging was a dark, violent opus of satanic majesty that would defy composition. In its final convulsion of agony, the tortured piano screamed for mercy.

"The Fairy's Picnic" screeched unsteadily to a halt. Carlotta leaned over and gave me a cobra-like stare that had petrified many a kid. She jabbed a finger into my ribs, perforating the green-paper elf vest. "I'm gonna pound the pee outta you."

The church erupted with applause. Miss Wigg, a shade whiter than the fairy's dress, sat frozen in the front pew, staring into space.

After the recital Carlotta asked me to step outside, but I took refuge at the reception in the church basement. She simmered down somewhat when she saw that the three of us and Miss Wigg were the star attractions. I couldn't even eat my jelly roll nor drink my Seven-Up with everyone shaking my hand.

Arne Salo paid us the ultimate compliment, "Sounded jus' like that music on 'Inner Sanctum.'"

Eunice LaPorte, Ishpeming's self-appointed fine arts critic, having gotten a college degree back in 1917, gushed over Miss Wigg. "Such primeval grandeur . . . the barbaric overtones . . . truly on the frontier of modern music. The sound effects by the children were particularly exciting. Tell me, my dear, what did you say the title was? Something about a picnic?"

Miss Wigg's eyes darted nervously around the room, her color just creeping back under the heavy layers of makeup. " . . . Yes . . . a picnic . . . it's called . . . 'The Witch's Picnic.'"

My right hand begged for relief, walking up and down the scale in the key of D for the forty-third time. This afternoon I had my first piano lesson since the recital, and Miss Wigg said I needed more discipline in my musical training. So tonight I was doing scales fifty times with each hand. She said it was good training, but I knew different. It was punishment, pure and simple. I couldn't figure out what she was so mad about. "The Witch's Picnic" had been a big hit, rescuing the recital from certain oblivion. As a matter of fact, she'd had an invitation to perform it at The Elks' Club in Marquette, but of course, "The Witch's Picnic" could never be played again, and she had to decline. Maybe that's why she was so mad.

Flushed with the success of the recital, my mother was really pumped up over my piano playing. The following Sunday I was booked to play scales at the Finnish Women's Coffee Club meeting at our house.

My plan had gone down in utter ruin. The prospects for a normal kid-hood were now nonexistent. I should have stepped outside the church with Carlotta. Perhaps I might have gotten lucky, and she would have broken a couple of my fingers.

I hurried through the last scale and, with a ragged sigh of relief, slid off the piano bench and turned on our four-foot-high Zenith radio just in time to catch the nightly adventures of "The Lone Ranger."

> . . . the masked man and Tonto leaped on their horses
> and galloped off in pursuit of the runaway stagecoach . . .

In the background drummed the now-familiar Lone Ranger theme—
The William Tell Overture—that never failed to bring goosebumps to my arms. Suddenly something jarred my consciousness—I cocked my ear to the radio. Could it be? Doing those scales, my brain had just been branded with the key of D. I jumped back on the piano bench and started fingering.

                                                      da—
                                             da—
                                    da—
Da—da—da da—da—da da—da

Gawd! That *was* it—it was in D—I was playing the Lone Ranger song! I quickly turned off the radio and went to work.

An hour later my mother came into the living room with a puzzled look. "You've been practicing all night. Are you sick?"

I looked up impatiently. "I'm okay. I just gotta finish up some work on this composition of mine."

She turned back toward the kitchen. "That sounds just like something I've heard on the radio."

Of course it does, I muttered under my breath. *Do you think piano players just play Miss Wigg's stupid songs all the time?*

With a flourish, I effortlessly rippled through the opening measures of the Lone Ranger theme over and over. By the stove, Teddy rolled over with a sleepy, contented groan and sank back into his dream, paws twitching in time to the music, running alongside the great horse Silver.

Boomer Jackson's Liberty Fire

As we heard the news, we skulked over to Smokey LaFarge's house in Frenchtown. It was dangerous since Frenchtown kids were inclined to throw large rocks at outsider kids. The three of us—Mutt Hukala, Reino Rovaniemi, and I—wanted to sneak a quick peek over Smokey's backyard fence and then hightail it out of there without being seen.

But Smokey spotted us. Deciding to really rub it in, he invited us into his yard where he cockily showed off what we had snuck over to see.

Four retreaded car tires, complete with inner tubes, were lying in the quack grass. The retreads were peeling off the tires like a snake shedding dead skin, and there were several lethal gashes in each tire carcass. The tubes were in shreds, looking like they had been chewed on by crazed beavers.

The three of us stared at them, open-mouthed. Anyone else would have thought this was worthless junk, but they would have been wrong. It was priceless treasure to every kid in town, and we had to choke back our envy.

It was early June 1944. My family was living in Milwaukee, but I was spending the summer with my grandmother in Republic, in Michigan's Upper Peninsula.

World War II rationing was still in full swing, and you rarely saw a tire, in *any* condition, that wasn't attached to someone's jalopy. But Smokey had *four* of them—*with inner tubes*. We didn't have to ask him where he got them—we already knew.

In a town the size of Republic, you couldn't trim your nose hairs without the word getting around, so when Porky Mattila blew all four tires at once on his '35 Ford, it was big news. Over the years, Porky had actually blown each of the Ford's tires several times. But new tires were expensive and almost impossible to get during the war, so he just kept patching the inner tubes and shoving boots in the tires when the holes got dangerously large. With all this extra reinforcement, the tires were unusually lumpy and tended to quiver and twitch when Porky drove the car. That didn't bother Porky—he quivered and twitched a lot, too.

The previous week on Memorial Day, after wiling away a beery afternoon at the Jack Pine Bar listening to the Indianapolis 500 on the bar radio, Porky decided he should practice for next year's 500 on the way out to his camp on the Dead Dog River. He tromped down on the gas pedal of the Ford and ended up taking the curve by Mattson's farm a little too fast. The car sailed off the road and landed in the south edge of Mattson's potato field. Porky was okay, but the impact was too much for the old tires and tubes. All of them were blown to smithereens. When his pit crew didn't show up to fix the tires, Porky got out of the car and staggered off to his camp to sleep off the beer. The next day he went back to the Ford in the potato field, and the car was sitting in the dirt on its brake drums. Four bare wheels were scattered alongside; all the tires and inner tubes were gone. Why would anyone steal tires that were so totally shot, he wondered.

Standing in the lush backyard quack grass, Smokey nudged one of the mangled tires with a ragged tennis shoe and chuckled in anticipation. "Betcha these babies'll smoke up the whole sky. They'll be able to see the Frenchtown fire all the way to Marquette."

Every Fourth of July the kids in Republic followed a popular town tradition: we lit bonfires at sunset. Nobody could remember how the idea started, but it was faithfully carried out every year. These were good-sized bonfires, so for weeks before the big day, kids scoured the town for paper, cardboard, and scraps of lumber.

Each neighborhood had its own bonfire. Mutt, Reino, and I were working on the bonfire in the East Kloman section; Smokey was the leader of the gang in charge of the Frenchtown bonfire. Frenchtown was our hated rival in all types of kid-hood contests, so there was fierce bonfire competition between us every year. The fires in other parts of town—Swedetown,

Park City, West Kloman—weren't as close as the Frenchtown fire and seemed less important.

The three of us stared at Smokey's tires with alarm. Up to now everyone had been satisfied with building fires with paper, cardboard, and wood. The bonfires were large but friendly—bright, warm flames flickering invitingly —mothers sitting on nearby blankets with little kids—men sucking beer out of cans and comparing each year's fire to bonfires of years past. But we were witnessing an ominous preview of things to come. With these tires, Smokey had brutally escalated the bonfire competition into a bonfire war. Clearly, from now on, anything combustible would be fair game.

Smokey sensed our discomfort and pressed his advantage. "Why don' you guys jus' give up this year an' come over an' take in *our* fire. It ought'a be sumthin'. I betcha this rubber'll smoke people out like rats. They'll come screamin' outta their houses, coughin'n chokin', har, har, har." Obviously, Smokey was losing touch with the true meaning of the Fourth of July.

It was hard to pass up watching a pile of tires and tubes burn, but we couldn't accept his offer. If we capitulated on the bonfire war, we would never be able to look the Frenchtown kids in the eye again.

Mutt put up a brave front, giving the nearest tire a disdainful kick. "This's small potatoes," he scoffed. "Wait'll ya see *our* fire. Prob'ly burn down two or three houses in East Kloman along with it."

Plucky words, but his voice lacked conviction.

Two weeks later Mutt and I were at the town dump, brushing away the big, blue-bottomed flies who found our slimy tennis shoes much more interesting than the garbage around us.

The East Kloman bonfire site was at the edge of town on the top of a large, smooth rock outcropping we called Bonfire Rock. The rock was ideal for a fire because there wasn't much of value nearby to catch fire. It was bordered by a field of tansy weeds, one of the town's graveled roads called Fire Street, and the dump—handy since most of our bonfire supplies came from the dump. With time running short, our gang had at least two guys stationed at the dump from dawn to dusk to snatch up any inflammable treasures as they were deposited by the garbage truck or the town merchants.

It was tough work—the dump long since picked clean of combustibles by the hordes of kids. Wood was scarce now since everybody in town was giving all their cast-off lumber to their own kids for the bonfires. The rats, resenting the invasion of their territory, squeaked and snarled indignantly as we waded through mountains of rotting potato peelings, egg shells, and grapefruit hulls just to snag an occasional cast-off Sears, Roebuck catalog.

Our haul for the day didn't amount to much—a stack of old *Mining Journal* newspapers, half a dozen egg cartons, and the bonanza of the day, two tomato crates from the Red Owl Store.

One night we had reconnoitered the Frenchtown bonfire site and discovered their truly fanatical dedication to building the biggest fire in the town's history. They had somehow managed to lay their hands on even more tires, and judging from the amount of good tread left on some of those tires, we concluded that the Frenchtown gang was not above lifting spares off parked cars.

Their bonfire fuel cache was a dark, foreboding mountain of tires and inner tubes expertly laced into a superstructure of lumber and tree branches. It loomed high into the air like a pregnant volcano, promising a fire that would cast a black oily cloud across the sky, darkening the earth for days to come.

While we had a respectable stockpile for our fire—a lot of paper, cardboard, vegetable crates, two-by-fours, and dead tree branches—it would not measure up against the Frenchtown bonfire. To save the reputation of the East Kloman gang we needed something really massive, highly combustible, and long-burning. But what?

Mutt and I heard the clinking of glass against glass and turned to see Boomer Jackson lurching down the road to perform his daily ritual of checking out the dump's inventory of bottles.

Boomer, a hobo who hung around Republic, was particularly partial to the homemade wine that Vito Spagarelli bootlegged in his basement. Vito gave a sizeable discount to anyone who furnished his own bottles, which is why Boomer prowled the dump. At all times his pockets were bulging with bottles of every imaginable type, all filled with Vito's wine.

Boomer was a major-league derelict—never sober—always with five- or six-weeks' growth of beard replete with remnants of his last fifty or so meals and wearing the same multi-layered, filthy clothes for years on end.

He would periodically hop a freight out of town in search of the Pacific Ocean. But every time he got past Duluth and ventured into North Dakota, where the land got flat, treeless, and generally alien-looking, he began to get depressed. Worse yet, he couldn't find any Italians out there to sell him wine, so he always returned to Republic. Because of this, the local wags started to call him Boomerang, eventually shortened to Boomer.

Curiously, he was fervently patriotic, always scouring the dump for yesterday's newspapers so he could read up on the war. The day after the Pearl Harbor bombing, Boomer marched into the U.S. Army recruiting office wanting to sign up. When they discovered that he had only three teeth, a variety of insect life in his body hair, and eleven bottles of bootleg wine squirreled away in his clothes, they threw him out.

Boomer wobbled up to us, casually removing a Heinz 57 catsup bottle out of a pocket. Putting the bottle up to his whiskery chops, he took a deep pull and with a satisfied belch slipped the bottle back into his pants. He gave our meager haul a bleary look. "Gonna have a good fire this year?"

"Not as good as Frenchtown," Mutt muttered dejectedly. "They gotta whole slew of tires down there. We ain't got nuthin' like that."

"Ties wud be good," Boomer said.

"What?"

"Railroad ties. Makes a good fire. Guy I met over near Ironwood used to carry an axe with him when he wuz ridin' th'freights. Every night he'd carve chips off th'railroad ties t'make a fire with. Burned like hell."

Mutt shook his head. "They catch us doin' that around here, an' we get our asses whipped fer sure. Besides, we need more'n chips."

Boomer reached into another pocket and pulled out a Sloan's Liniment bottle. After a healthy slug, he smiled slyly. "I know where there's a heap a railroad ties jus' goin' t'waste."

Mutt and I perked up. "Where?" I asked.

"Coupl'a miles th'other side a Pump House Lake."

Mutt jumped up. "Show us."

The sun was getting low, but the heat of the day still caused the crickets to shrill mercilessly in the tall weeds by the railroad tracks. The three of us walked between the rails, Mutt setting an impatient fast pace.

Boomer's raggedy, baggy clothes clinked merrily as he tried to keep up, even though he was the only one who knew exactly where we were going. We were now about three miles east of town. I couldn't remember being this far out since it was well past our usual fishing spots.

Boomer pointed up the tracks ahead of us. "That's where they are."

We stopped at a spot along the tracks where the ground sloped steeply down on one side. About twenty feet below us, near a clump of spruce, was a huge heap of loose railroad ties which appeared to have been dumped from the track bed. They were in tough shape—badly cracked and covered with mildew.

Boomer pulled out a Milk of Magnesia bottle and took a big gulp. "Years ago they fixed this section a track . . . replaced the ties. Didn't have any use fer th'old ones, so they jus' threw 'em down there."

We scrambled down the slope to get a better look. Mutt shook his head. Poking a mildewed tie, he said, "Don' look like they'd burn too good. Lookit that gunk."

Boomer snorted. "Ya don' know much 'bout railroad ties, do ya? They's soaked with creosote. You could leave 'em in a lake fer years, an' they'd still burn."

"What's creosote?" Mutt asked.

"Don' know 'xackly . . . keeps th'wood from rotting, though. Makes it burn like hell, too."

Mutt fingered the ties, not saying anything further. Boomer may have been a low-life, wino bum, but no one would ever question his knowledge regarding anything to do with railroads.

Boomer continued. "If ya kin lug a coupl'a those inta town, ya'll have yerself a nice fire."

The tower of ties looked like a pile of giant Pick-Up Sticks. There must have been a hundred or more. "A couple?" Mutt exclaimed. "Why not take 'em *all?*"

Boomer idly scratched his crotch, pondering that idea for several seconds. He gazed off into the distance, mentally picturing a mountain of blazing railroad ties. His dirty, unshaven face cracked into a cunning grin, exposing the three lonesome yellow teeth. "Let's do 'er!" he cried.

Grunting with exertion, we lifted one of the ties, Boomer on one end, with Mutt and me on the other. I had lived around the tracks all my life, but I'd never realized just how big a railroad tie was. It was a monumental struggle to get it up the slope to the tracks, but that was nothing compared to carrying it the three miles into town. Boomer sobered up several times on the way, and we had to keep stopping while he refueled from one of his many bottles. My arm and leg muscles were screaming, and both hands were throbbing with splinters by the time we got the railroad tie to the edge of town.

Boomer had been reading up on the recent D-Day operation at Normandy and was fully aware of the tactical importance of surprise. He declared that we should hide the ties in the tansy weeds just below Bonfire Rock. "It's gonna take us awhile to lug them ties in, an' we don't wanna tip off the Frenchtown gang what we got here." With a conspiratorial gleam in his bloodshot eyes he added, "This's our secret weapon, an' we ain't gonna spring it on 'em till th'last minute."

Early the next morning we pounded on doors and rounded up every kid in East Kloman for the brutal task ahead. Work gloves were scrounged out of woodsheds. Thermos bottles were filled with Kool-Aid. Peanut butter and jelly sandwiches were wrapped in waxed paper and stuffed into pockets. Boomer had topped off all of his bottles the night before in Vito's Spagarelli's basement.

The whole gang quickly marched off down the railroad tracks, and in less than an hour, we reached the cache of railroad ties. Excitement soared when the rest of the kids, looking at the pile of ties, realized the magnitude of the project we were undertaking.

Because of his railroad experience, Boomer wisely pronounced himself supervisor—dividing us into work groups, selecting the ties, and generally avoiding the grunt work. We trooped back down the tracks toward town like a column of ants, four kids to each railroad tie. All day long we shuttled back and forth between the pile of ties and the weeds next to Bonfire Rock.

In the middle of the afternoon a freight train came rumbling toward us as we were hauling a load of ties into town. We stepped off the tracks and waited for it to pass. As the locomotive rolled by, the engineer, open-mouthed, gawked down at us holding the railroad ties and squinted apprehensively at the tracks ahead of him.

By suppertime, we had deposited a dozen railroad ties in the tansy weeds below Bonfire Rock. We were dirty, full of splinters, and dog-tired.

To a casual observer it was nothing more than a large pile of scroungy, busted-up pieces of moldy wood—to us it was the ultimate weapon that was going to decide the bonfire war.

*The engineer, open-mouthed, gawked down at us
holding the railroad ties.*

It took almost two weeks of unbelievable sweat and strain, but we finally got all the railroad ties to Bonfire Rock. Boomer's strategy of hiding the ties in the weeds was brilliant, because on July third, the day after we finished the hauling, the Frenchtown gang conducted a spying mission of their own. Smokey and a couple of his henchmen casually wandered over to Bonfire Rock where Mutt, Reino, Boomer, and I were sitting, picking wood splinters out of our hands.

Smokey spat arrogantly on our pile of paper, wood, and cardboard that we had left in place to throw off snooping outsiders. "Whaddaya gonna have here, a marshmallow roast? Ya better hope it ain't cold tomorrow night, 'cause this fire ain't gonna be big enough t'warm yer ass, har, har, har."

Reino couldn't stand it and jumped up from where he was sitting next to Boomer. "Oh, yeah? Jus' wait till tomorr . . ."

Boomer quickly stuck out his foot and knocked Reino's legs out from under him. "Hah! Gotcha good, Reino." Theatrically, he hiccuped and gave us a loose-lipped, drunken grin.

But Boomer wasn't drunk. He'd eased up on the boozing during the two weeks we were hauling ties. In fact, I hadn't seen him take a drink at all in the last two or three days. The whites of his eyes no longer had that bloodshot roadmap texture—he didn't clink anymore when he walked—it was eerie.

Smokey and his cronies left in high spirits, assured that victory was theirs. After all, we only had a puny pile of assorted trash for our bonfire and were wasting our time horsing around with the town drunk.

Mutt had picked up on Boomer's act to shut Reino up. "Boomer, you ain't drinkin', huh? Ain't seen you take a drink all day."

Boomer glanced around to make sure Smokey was out of earshot. He leaned in toward us and whispered hoarsely. "This ain't no time fer gettin' drunk. Ya think it's gonna be easy puttin' all those ties together t'make a bonfire? Hell, no! It'll take a real job of engineerin', but I'm jus' the guy t'show ya how t'do it. We gotta get up real early tomorrow, 'cause it'll take us all day." He leaned back on the rock, propping his body up on his ragged elbows, staring at us with an intentness I had never seen in his eyes before. "Ah . . . but when we get 'er all t'gether and torch it, yer gonna see one hell-uva blaze. Yessir . . . one fer the books. The Frenchtown kids'll wanna piss on their fire when they see this one. Now you guys go home'n get a good night's sleep, so's we kin get an early start tomorrow."

The Fourth of July dawned windless and clear with the promise of a scorching hot day. I jumped out of bed and gulped down a bowl of Wheaties before running over to pick up Mutt and Reino. We charged off to Bonfire Rock, eagerly anticipating the big day. From way off we could see Boomer standing alone on the rock waiting for us.

Boomer was alert and cold sober. As the rest of the kids showed up, he started issuing orders with the precision of a field commander. In fact, Mutt started calling him *General* Boomer, and the other kids picked it up. Boomer laughed, but you could see that he was lapping up the recognition of his leadership.

He had several coils of clothesline to be used for tying the railroad ties together. When we asked where he got the clothesline, Boomer just smiled. A lot of housewives were going to be furious the next time they went out into the backyard to hang up the wash.

Laboriously, we began to haul the ties up from the weeds to the top of Bonfire Rock, Boomer directing us on how to arrange them around the heap of paper, cardboard, and wood. This stuff, which Smokey thought was the totality of our bonfire fuel, was merely going to serve as kindling.

As the day wore on, the pile of railroad ties grew higher and higher. Although the pile looked like a random heap of wood, each tie had been strategically placed for maximum burning efficiency. Boomer had expertly lashed them together with the clothesline to keep them firmly in place.

By late afternoon we had all the ties on the pile. The whole thing was about as big as a good-sized garage—more than fifteen feet across—about twelve feet high. It looked like a house for a giant beaver. All the kids stared at it in awe. *We were going to burn this?*

Everyone raced home to bolt down supper, except Boomer who wandered off toward the middle of town. Before sunset all the kids were gathered back at the rock, anxious to torch the bonfire. But since Boomer had become our de facto leader, no one dared light it until he got there. Grownups began to drift up to the rock with blankets, beer, and pop. Some brought marshmallows and wieners for roasting.

Just before dark, Boomer finally showed up—except from the neck up it didn't look like Boomer at all. He had gone to Sullivan's Barber Shop and splurged on *the works.* Sullivan had given him a brand-new head—his hair was trimmed and combed—the scraggly whiskers were gone—his face was scrubbed pink.

He was carrying an open bottle of chilled champagne from Nardi's Liquor Store. It was *real* champagne in a *real* champagne bottle. Nobody had ever seen Boomer with a bottle whose contents actually matched the label. In the breast pocket of his ragged suit coat he'd stuck a small American flag. Boomer had spared no expense to celebrate the Fourth of July in style.

Folks couldn't decide which was more incredible, the giant beaver house made out of railroad ties, or Boomer's new head. Some of the guys really gave him the business.

"Boomer, you tryin' t'charm one of th'town girls into ridin' the freight out t'Duluth with ya?"

"Hey, Boomer! Did Sullivan haf'ta to beat your hair clippings to death on his shop floor?"

Boomer took it all in good humor with a grand smile on his new face, sipping champagne from the bottle.

Realizing that the fire could be started now that Boomer was here, the kids started pestering him to put a match to it. Boomer held up his hand for quiet. "We're gonna give Frenchtown th'first shot. Then we'll light ours an' show 'em what a *real* fire looks like.

Bugsy Maki, one of our gang, edged timidly up to Boomer. Bugsy was a few years older than the rest of us but slow-witted. He was good at working with his hands, and he liked to take stuff from the dump and make presents for people. Bugsy put something glittery in Boomer's hand. It was a medal made out of the shiny bottom of a beer can with two strips of red ribbon glued to it. Attached was a long loop of twine for hanging the medal around his neck.

"For you, General Boomer," he said in his soft, hesitating voice. "For helpin' us with the fire we're goin' t'have here tonight."

Boomer looked at Bugsy for several seconds, acknowledged his thanks with a silent nod, and took the medal and put the loop over his head. His eyes were glistening.

"Frenchtown's lit their fire!" Reino cried, pointing off to the north. Sure enough, a plume of greasy, black smoke from the burning tires boiled into the evening sky blotting out the sunset reflecting off the wispy clouds. Even from half a mile away we could see huge orange flames licking at the mass of tires. It was a great fire, one of the best I'd seen.

Boomer wasn't impressed. "Ya call *that* a fire?" he blared out, taking a large swig of champagne. "That's nuthin' but a li'l pussycat spark. I build bigger campfires than that when I'm on th'road ridin' freights!" Wild-eyed, he turned to the East Kloman gang. "We'll show 'em a fire, right boys?" We echoed his sentiment with a chorus of yells.

Boomer produced a box of wooden matches, gave a handful of matches to Mutt, Reino, and me, then addressed the crowd. "My lootennants here have the job a lightin' the official 1944 East Kloman Fourth a July bonfire."

It was a magnificent honor, not to be taken lightly. I took the matches and walked slowly and ceremoniously up to the railroad ties, savoring the thrill of the moment. The twilight was darkening rapidly now, and the ties were silhouetted against the western sky, towering over me like rubble from some immense, collapsed wooden skyscraper.

I struck a match on the rock. It flared and went out. Nervously, I struck another and cupped it with my other hand. Boomer had left wads of newspaper at the edge of the ties to get the fire started, so I lit some of them. Mutt and Reino were around the other side doing the same thing.

It took awhile, but after several minutes the kindling in the center caught fire. When the ties ignited, the flames lit up the whole area. The crowd on Bonfire Rock clapped their hands in appreciation. Beer cans were opened. Little kids ran off to find roasting sticks.

But this was not going to be a marshmallow and wiener fire. As the creosote reached its critical temperature, the fire began to hiss ominously. Sharp, pistol-shot noises cracked from the flaming ties.

Suddenly, the fire shifted into high gear. The hiss grew to a breathy roar like some night creature with an infinite lung capacity exhaling on the crowd. The flames shot way up into the darkness, spiralling embers further into the sky and lighting up all of East Kloman. All the railroad ties were blazing now, and a heavy wall of heat forced us back from the fire.

Boomer stood transfixed, staring into the fire and taking huge, frequent gulps of champagne. This was the first time he'd had anything to drink in a week or more, and he was making up for lost time. He lurched over to the edge of Bonfire Rock and yelled to the north where the Frenchtown fire was still blazing.

"HOW D'YA LIKE *THIS* FIRE, FRENCHTOWN?"

In fact, there was no comparison. Even at this distance, we could easily see that the Frenchtown fire was dwarfed by the enormous blaze we had going. Boomer cackled with glee and did a little jig on the rock with his champagne bottle.

The rest of us were silent, mesmerized by the size and intensity of the fire. Finally, Chunky O'Neill, an eight-year-old endowed with more guts than good sense, impaled a marshmallow on a three-foot stick and charged toward the fire. Before he even got close, the terrific heat slowed Chunky to a stop. He stuck the marshmallow on the stick out toward the fire, and with eyes closed and head turned to shield his face, he edged forward. The marshmallow was blackened when it was still a good six feet away from the flames.

"Lookit that, would'ja?" Boomer marvelled, gazing up at the flames which were now over a hundred feet in the air. "I bet'cha they kin see this in Marquette . . . maybe even Chicago."

The flames responded by leaping higher. Boomer was ecstatic—the Frenchtown fire was now forgotten. He finished off the champagne and flung the empty bottle far into the tansy weeds. "Hell," he cried. "They're prob'ly see'n it over in France where our boys is fightin' fer liberty!" He paused dramatically and began to pace back and forth like a preacher addressing his congregation. "Tha's what this is . . . a *Liberty Fire* . . . and by golly, I helped build 'er!" He continued on, now babbling loudly to no one in particular. "This'll show 'em. They wouldn't lemme in the army to go over there t'fight. I begged 'em to take me, but they wouldn't do 'er. But now I'm sendin' a message. I'm here, you guys, an' I'm proud t'be an' American. I can't be there with ya, but I'm cheerin' ya on!"

Several of us kids stood at attention with eyes fixed on the fire. I could hear "The Battle Hymn of the Republic" playing in my head.

The fire was now creating a nasty backdraft, sucking air into itself to feed on the oxygen. A piece of butcher paper that someone had dropped from a pound of wieners skittered along the rock and whipped into the fire.

"What in hell you kids gone an' done?" somebody bellowed. Jake Hovi, one of the township volunteer firemen, had scrabbled up on Bonfire Rock and was looking at the fire with extreme consternation. "Jeezus, whaddaya burnin' there? Railroad ties? The fire's too big. We gotta put this thing out before it sets fire t'something."

"What's gonna catch on fire?" Mutt asked. "The nearest house is way down there. Ain't nuthin' up here but this rock, the dump, an' a big field of tansy weeds."

But Jake liked to play fireman. He'd probably never seen a blaze like this one, and he wasn't going to be denied the chance to put it out. He snapped his fingers authoritatively at some of the men standing on the rock. "Get some buckets a water up here an' douse this thing right now!"

Three or four of the guys who lived nearby reluctantly put down their beer cans, tore themselves away from the hypnotizing fire, and climbed down from the rock to get buckets.

Boomer rushed up to Jake and grabbed his arm. "Nooooooo, . . . don't put it out," he howled. "Don'cha see? It's the Fourth of July, an' this here's the Liberty Fire."

"Gitcher hands off me, ya filthy drunk," Jake snapped.

"Please let 'er be." Boomer pleaded. "This fire's the first good thing I built since I dunno when."

Jake snorted and turned away. He marched over to the edge of the rock, waiting for the buckets to arrive. Boomer turned to the fire and looked at it in loving dismay.

In a few minutes the guys returned with buckets of water. They scrabbled across the rock but had to stop about eight feet from the flames. The heat was just too intense. They threw the water as far as they could, but it only reached the fringes of the fire. The Liberty Fire belched a few unconcerned clouds of steam and kept on burning fiercely. Boomer sat on the rock and moaned.

Now Jake really got irritated and ordered more water to be brought up. But the result was the same. Finally, in frustration he grabbed one of the full buckets. "Yer doin' it all wrong. *I'll* show ya how t'throw water." He stepped purposefully toward the Liberty Fire and flung the water high in the air.

The water hit the fire. With an ugly, loud crack and a cloud of steam, it lashed back violently, sending large flying embers in all directions. One of them landed on the front of Jake's white shirt, scorching a hole clear through to the skin. Jake yelped and tore open his shirt, brushing his chest furiously.

Boomer, standing back from the action, cried out, "Don'cha see? Ya *can't* put out the Liberty Fire."

In a rage, Jake stalked over to Boomer. "I'll put *you* out," he rasped and gave Boomer a swift punch to the face. Boomer went down, blood spurting from his nose and mouth.

Everybody became totally still. The women were shocked. Guys held cans of beer but weren't drinking. The Liberty Fire raged on, throwing flickering light on Boomer and Jake. Boomer's blood dripped on the rock, turning black in the strange light.

Boomer put his hands flat on the rock and started to get to his feet. Jake kicked him in the ribs, and he went down again. A swift backdraft from the fire sprang up, fluttering Jake's shirt tail. Some guy, I don't know who it was, tried to wrap his arms around Jake and pull him away, but Jake shook him off.

Eyes shut, Boomer grimaced with pain but got slowly to his feet. He spat out one of his three remaining teeth. Jake was smirking now and reached out for Boomer's medal.

"Whazzis?" he laughed. "You taking arts'n crafts classes at the town dump?" He jerked the medal off Boomer's neck.

It happened so fast that nobody really saw the punch coming. Boomer hit Jake with a lightning right cross to the side of the head that sent him sprawling. The medal clattered across the rock. Boomer straightened up to his full height. He had always walked sort of hunched over, and I never realized he was so tall. He was cold sober by now, and the light of the fire made him look different somehow.

"You can't put *me* out," he said to Jake in a steady voice that carried over the roar of the fire, "and you sure as hell ain't gonna put out the Liberty Fire."

Guys laughed at that, breaking the tension. The buckets were put down and more beer cans popped open

Boomer bent down, picked up his medal, and strode off Bonfire Rock.

The Liberty Fire burned for four days. Mutt and I went up to look at it on the fourth day, and it was much smaller. Even in its reduced state, the remaining coals still threw out a lot of heat. While we were standing there, Chunky O'Neill came by with some more marshmallows, determined to get them roasted. We ran him off. Nobody was going to roast marshmallows over the Liberty Fire.

We never saw Boomer again. We later heard that he had been spotted around the train depot the night of the Fourth about the time a midnight westbound freight was due. After a couple of months, folks figured that Boomer must have made it all the way across North Dakota.

That winter, when the first blizzard hit, people gathered around heaters in Chub's Standard Station, the Red Owl Store, the four-lane bowling alley, and other places where people gather when the weather is cold. They wondered where Boomer was. A lot of them were convinced that Boomer was somewhere out on the West Coast soaking up the sunshine. Others said that he was probably in Mexico chasing senoritas. There were even some who thought he had managed to get into the army and was over in Europe mopping up the Nazis and would probably marry some French woman who owned a vineyard. Wherever he was, I'll bet he was still wearing the beer-can medal and telling everybody all about the night of the big Liberty Fire.

The Hero

When you're a kid, there's nothing worse than changing schools in the middle of the year. Just when you think you've figured out what the teachers are trying to drill into your head, your family up and moves and you have to wade in and try to make some sense out of whatever they're teaching in the new school. To make matters worse, all the boys—some of the girls, too—in the new school want to see how tough you are. There are so many after-school fights you need an appointment book to schedule them.

It was April 1945. My parents had given up their World War II defense jobs in downtown Milwaukee and had just begun working at Green Knolls, an exclusive country club designed for the recreation and amusement of Milwaukee's brewery magnates. It was on the fringes of the city—too far to commute—so we lived with the other employees right at the club.

Jersey Junction Elementary was the only grade school in the area—a tiny, two-classroom school at a remote crossroad in this dairy-farming region west of Milwaukee. One room housed the first through third grades, and the other was for the fourth, fifth, and sixth grades. I couldn't help but wonder how much I was going to learn with a bunch of weasel-faced fourth- and fifth-graders in the same room, whining over the unreasonableness of long division and the spelling of two-syllable words.

Early Monday morning—the air was thick with erasers and spit-balls—girls giggling and screaming—boys huddled furtively in the back of the classroom, swapping dirty jokes. Leaning against the wall by the door, I was trying to look inconspicuous while waiting for a teacher to show up.

45

Just when I was about to dissolve into a puddle of sweat, the teacher marched in. A no-nonsense, battle-hardened veteran of the grade-school wars, she silenced the room with an imperious glare over steel-rimmed reading glasses.

"Good morning. Before we get started, I want to introduce a new student. He's just transferred from the Kilbourn Street School in downtown Milwaukee and will be joining the sixth-graders. Please welcome Gerald Harju to Jersey Junction Elementary School." She pointed a finger at me.

The girls tittered. Older boys sneered and snorted. Flinty eyes sized me up for a pounding at recess.

Sure enough, at the mid-morning recess some farm-boy thug, who no doubt kept in shape by bench-pressing dairy cows, swaggered up to me in the yard with an entourage of toadies in his wake. His Neanderthaloid head—a jaw twice as wide as his sloping forehead—towered over me as he fired off the opening salvo of the new-kid-persecution ritual.

"Har-ju? Har-yoo? I'm fine. How *are you*? Heh, heh, heh." He paused to let the others appreciate his cleverly crafted pun on my name and to see how I would react.

At the age of twelve, I wasn't exactly a physical force to be reckoned with—about two inches shorter than the average girl my age, with a lot of residual baby fat here and there. Therefore, any physical confrontation deserved serious consideration. I had three choices: take a poke at him and die a violent death; walk away, thereby permanently branding myself as a chicken-livered yellow-belly; or talk my way out of it.

"Heard it before," I remarked offhandedly.

"Heard whut before?"

"'Harju . . . I'm fine . . . How *are you*?' Lots'a kids've come up with that one." I was hoping that a little friendly chat might lead to a stimulating conversation on the ethnic background of my name and he would forget about pounding the pee out of me.

I was wrong. He stepped in close and started punching a hole in my breastbone by jabbing me with a grimy finger. I could smell the cow manure on his shoes.

"How wud ya like it if I ripped yer butt off an' handed it to ya so's ya cud look at it real close?"

That was a pretty good one, I thought, and I was hastily thinking up a snappy comeback when we were conveniently interrupted.

Oblivious to the impending bloodshed, a fortyish balding guy in a sweatshirt and tennis shoes, with a chrome whistle hanging around his neck, strode up and slapped a friendly hand on my shoulder.

"Is this the new boy?" he said, with an engaging toothy grin. "I'm Mr. Peeples, the physical education teacher—the kids call me Coach," he continued, extending his hand which I gratefully shook. "I also teach geography," he reluctantly admitted, as though geography was a minor eddy in the otherwise smooth mainstream of his life's pursuits.

Disappointed at being deprived of witnessing my demise, the gang of boys drifted off.

"I'm sure glad to have you on board," Peeples went on enthusiastically. "We need every red-blooded boy we can get our hands on for the Jersey Junction team."

"What team is that?" I asked.

"Why, the softball team, of course . . . the Jersey Junction Badgers. I'm the coach. Gotta good team this year . . . won our first two games. Y'know that big boy you were just making friends with? Heinrich Blunt . . . our star heavy hitter. Hit four home runs in the last game we played. We've got a good chance of taking the Packawaunee Pony League championship this year."

His expression faded to somberness. "Problem is, we don't have enough older boys to put on the field." He leaned toward me in embarrassed confidentiality and lowered his voice. "Right now, we have to use three *girls* to field a full team. I don't have to tell you what kind of razzing I get from the other coaches. Y'know what I mean?"

I nodded my head vigorously. Playing ball with girls was something to be avoided at all costs.

"Have you played softball before?" Peeples asked.

I didn't even know what softball was. I'd lived most of my life in Upper Michigan, where organized sports for grade-school kids was nonexistent. With the limited resources we had, we played a curious version of baseball which we called street-ball.

Street-ball was played on side streets where traffic was light. Parked cars or street lights were used as bases. We relied heavily on black electrical tape to hold our equipment together. The surface of the ball—originally a baseball—had long since submerged beneath layers of this tape used to keep the cover on. As the bats got splintered, they were taped up. The kids who were lucky enough to have gloves had to tape them to keep the stuffing from falling out.

"I've played some ball," I answered.

"Good, good. What position do you play?" Peeples asked.

That was an interesting question. Street-ball had very fluid fielding assignments, since we didn't have teams. A kid batted and ran the base paths until he made an out. Then he was sentenced to the outfield, rotating to different positions—outfield, infield, pitcher—as other batters made out, until he came up to bat again.

"I've played all positions," I told Peeples modestly.

Peeples' face split into a wide grin. "Excellent! Be at ball practice after the last class tomorrow afternoon. Here's what we'll do. We'll try you out at each of the positions that the girls are currently playing to see where you're best suited. A couple of these girls aren't bad, but softball's a *man's* game . . . you know what I mean? Don't worry. You'll be in the starting line-up of the Jersey Junction Badgers for the next game."

I was quickly recaptured by Heinrich and his Huns before recess was over. Since time was running short, they had to let me off with one of their more lenient initiations—carrying me over to the water fountain on the outside wall and setting me down on the running water to soak my crotch. I laughed this off good-naturedly, comfortable with the knowledge that these boys—my future fellow teammates—would shortly get to know and respect me.

The next afternoon, Peeples stood at home plate with a bat in one hand. He blew his whistle sharply to start infield practice. This consisted of hitting ground balls to the third baseman, shortstop, and second baseman, who would then throw it over to the first baseman—me. Peeples had benched the girl first baseman so he could try me out for the job.

"Okay, third base," Peeples barked. He flipped the softball in the air and hit a sharp ground ball to Heinrich Blunt, the third baseman. Blunt scooped up the grounder easily, cocked his eight-foot-long King Kong arm, and threw the ball over to first base.

Most projectiles have an arc—first they go up and then they go down. This ball ripped across the diamond on a completely horizontal path, frying air molecules as it went. I watched in horror as it bore down on me. In that minuscule moment I knew I was in a league several light-years up from street-ball.

My body instinctively shifted into basic survival mode. I ducked. The ball screamed by and hit the side of the school building, chipping out several bricks.

Peeples smiled at me good-naturedly. "Fielding's a little rusty, huh? Just relax. It'll come back to you."

More ground balls were hit. I mustered up enough courage to try catching the throws, but the ones that didn't completely whistle past me smashed into my sad, old street-ball glove with terrible force, sending stuffing and tape fragments flying before the ball dropped to the ground. This was *soft*ball?

Catching a ball in street-ball had been simple. It was soft and spongy from old age and layers of tape and was extremely sticky from the adhesive. You couldn't drop it if you tried. Even if you totally misjudged the ball's trajectory, you still had a second chance by snagging one of the pieces of unravelled tape that were trailing along behind the ball. But the softball—a gross misnomer—was big, hard, and slick. There was no margin for error.

My problem wasn't helped a bit by the regular first baseman, Gertrude Schultz, a sturdy, rosy-cheeked Wisconsin farm girl with the physique and temperament of a rhinoceros. She didn't appreciate being sidelined while I tried out for her position. She sulked behind first base, pawing impatiently at the grass as she critiqued my play.

"Where'd you learn t'play ball, ya li'l cow turd?" she bellowed. "My dog can catch a ball better'n that."

Blunt's arm was now fully warmed up. He scooped up one of Peeples' grounders and launched a particularly wicked rocket-throw over to me. It blasted by me before I got my glove up. Gertrude, standing ten feet behind me, speared it bare-handed.

Peeples thought it prudent to put Gertrude back at first base. He proceeded to try me out as catcher—one of the other positions held by a girl. Irene Suggs, the regular catcher, scowled menacingly from the sideline as I squatted down behind home plate at the start of batting practice. I squinted apprehensively at the pitcher through the iron bars on the catcher's mask.

I had never worn a catcher's mask before. In fact, there was no catcher in street-ball since there were never enough kids to play all nine positions. If a street-ball batter didn't like the looks of the pitch coming in, he simply dropped the bat, caught the ball himself, and threw it back to the pitcher.

The Jersey Junction pitcher wheeled into his windup and pitched the ball underhand toward home plate. The pitch came in slower than the throws from the infielders that I had been unsuccessfully trying to catch at first base. This was more like it, I thought, as I concentrated on catching the ball. I wanted to recoup some semblance of respect after my disastrous try-out at first base.

The pitch was high, but that didn't stop the overeager kid in the batter's box who took a looping, uppercut swing at the ball and missed. I flinched.

Luckily, I was wearing the catcher's mask. The ball sailed unimpeded over my glove and slammed in between the bars on the mask, coming to rest a whisker from the tip of my nose.

The pitcher rolled his eyes in disgust. Kids hooted and laughed. Peeples slowly walked toward home plate.

So I became the right fielder. Right field—the root cellar of the ball-diamond—was the repository for players who might do irreparable harm playing any other position.

Nothing was ever hit to right field. In those days, all kids—even left-handers—batted right-handed; consequently, all the balls were hit to left or center field. Left fielders and center fielders were expected to snag screaming line drives off their shoe tops or scoop up solid hits on the first bounce and quickly fire the ball into second base to keep the runner from stretching a single into a double. They had to be able to leap high in the air to catch towering shots near the fence, thereby robbing the opposition of certain home runs.

But nothing of that nature was required to play right field. Lots of right fielders became gardeners or horticulturists in later life because they developed such a keen interest in watching the grass and flowers grow while they waited for the opposing team to make their three outs. No athletic skill tryouts were required to play right field because it had already been determined that you didn't *have* any athletic skills.

*The ball sailed unimpeded over my glove and slammed in
between the bars on the mask, coming to rest a
whisker from the tip of my nose.*

But Peeples had kept his promise about making me one of the starting nine of the Jersey Junction Badgers, and right field or not, I was grateful just to be on the team. As I walked back to the Green Knolls Country Club after softball practice, I was deep in thought, trying to figure out how I could separate five dollars from my old man so I could buy a new glove.

A bicycle rider passed me, then screeched to a halt and turned around. A girl I vaguely remembered from school jumped off her bike and began walking beside me.

"Hi, remember me? I'm Cora Flug." She was shaped like a fire hydrant—short and pudgy—with twin pigtails and wire-rimmed glasses.

I nodded politely, eyeing a new Joe DiMaggio fielding glove in the wire handlebar basket on her bike.

"I guess you're gonna take my place in right field," she said. "It's okay . . . I'm not very good at softball anyway."

Then I remembered. She was the one Peeples had benched in order to put me in right field. I hadn't noticed her much during practice, but then, who notices right fielders? Cora Flug was the third girl—my last chance to make the team. I didn't know what to say.

Finally, I muttered, "Wanna sell that glove?" reasoning that I might get a good deal on it since she wouldn't be needing it anymore.

She shook her head. "No . . . I don't think so . . . my father bought it for me. He's really the one who wanted me to play on the team. Said it was a family tradition."

"Tradition?"

"Yeah. He played ball at Jersey Junction when he was a kid."

This conversation wasn't going anywhere, and since I normally didn't make a habit of talking to girls anyway, I nodded again and kept walking.

She got on her bike and began to pedal in a circle around me. "I was watching when Coach was trying you out at first base. Those infielders throw *real* hard, don't they?"

I kept walking.

"Maybe you and me could get together sometime after school," she added. "I could throw the ball, and you could practice your catching."

I kept walking.

That Saturday the Jersey Junction Badgers took on the Roquefort Corners Elementary School Fighting Guinea Pigs, a team with dubious prospects, featuring six pint-sized fourth-graders in the starting line-up. The Badgers showed the Guinea Pigs no mercy, pulverizing them thirty-seven to two. The Guinea Pigs did their only scoring in the first inning when our pitcher had trouble adjusting to their two-inch-high strike zone and walked in two runs. Needless to say, I didn't see any action in right field.

Blunt had a big day at the plate, blasting six home runs. Gertrude had a triple and two doubles, and Irene, two doubles and three singles. Of course, Peeples had the two girls at the bottom of the batting roster for the simple reason that they were girls.

Even if I was doomed to obscurity playing right field, I would most certainly get into the Packawaunee Pony League record books. In our monster second inning when the Badgers scored seventeen runs, I single-handedly strangled the rally by making all three outs, striking out each time at bat.

I had never been able to hit, but in street-ball—not a team sport—nobody cared. Every kid was waiting for his turn at bat, and if you were an easy out, so much the better—everyone else got their turns quicker. In fact, good hitters were a liability because they monopolized the bat. Needless to say, I had been in great demand for street-ball games.

The Jersey Junction Badgers took an entirely different view of my hitting skills. After the game Blunt commented that we would have scored *at least* twenty-five runs in that second inning if it hadn't been for my strikeouts. There was some talk about setting me back on the water fountain to refocus my attention.

I was trudging dejectedly back to the country club when Cora Flug rode up on her bike. During the game, she had been the lone voice in the crowd cheering me on when I was at bat.

She walked her bicycle alongside. "You need help," she said matter-of-factly. "Come over to our place tomorrow. My daddy can give you some pointers."

Sunday afternoon, I took Cora up on her invitation and went over to the Flug dairy farm—about a mile from Green Knolls Country Club. Cora and her father were sitting on the front porch. She must have taken after her mother, because she certainly didn't resemble her father. A huge man, Homer Flug had piercing Ty Cobb eyes set deep in a bronzed face and hands the size of baseball mitts.

"Cora tells me ya wanna learn hittin'," he said, shifting a major-league cud of chewing tobacco to his other cheek and accurately hitting a spittoon near the porch railing.

"Yessir. I'm pretty rotten."

"Well . . . let's see what we can do." He produced a softball and bat, and we went down to the big red barn. Homer gave me the bat and stood me next to the barn wall.

"Okay, I'll pitch a few to ya. We'll see what yer doin' wrong."

Homer stepped away about forty feet and faced me. I stood over an imaginary home plate and waggled the bat. He assumed a professional pitcher's stance—the ball in his right hand behind his back—leaning over at the waist—staring down at me with intense concentration. He went into a furious windmill windup and flung an underhanded pitch. It steamed in at my head. I hit the dirt—or what passed for dirt at a dairy farm—and the ball cracked into the barn wall.

Ohmigawd! I know what he's doing. He's trying to kill me so Cora can get back into right field.

"Arm's a li'l cold," Homer commented dryly. "I'll get 'er in there in a minute."

I picked up the ball and threw it back to him. He put up one of his mammoth paws to catch it. The ball smacked into his open palm and dropped to the ground.

His next pitch sailed five feet over my head. This time when I threw the ball back, it hit his thumb, and he winced in pain.

"It's been awhile since I played," he remarked. "But it'll come back t'me."

Homer threw about fifteen pitches, and none came close to the strike zone. Finally, I put the bat down. "You used to play for the Jersey Junction School?" I asked.

Homer smiled nostalgically. "You bet'cha. I was the right fielder."

After several more wild pitches, Homer said something about milking some cows and wandered off.

"I thought you said he could give me some pointers," I whispered to Cora.

"He never told me he was a right fielder," she whispered back.

The next game was against the Peevey Elementary School Woodchucks. The Woodchucks fielded a better team than the Guinea Pigs, but we still whipped them soundly, fifteen to seven.

Cora decided to lend me her Joe DiMaggio glove to atone for her father's inability to give me any help the previous Sunday. It was a dandy glove, but it made no difference—nothing was hit to right field.

I extended my no-hitting streak to fourteen—more noteworthy because they were all strikeouts. I tried everything to break out of the slump—swinging slower—swinging faster—swinging up on the ball—swinging down on the ball. Nothing worked.

A right fielder who can't hit leads a lonely life. None of my teammates talked to me—actually keeping their distance for fear that whatever was afflicting my hitting might be contagious. Even Peeples, who had been so adamant about getting me on the team, didn't have much to say. Of course, he had problems of his own. He was already concentrating on next Saturday's game against the Hickory Hills Falcons.

Hickory Hills was an exclusive, rolling wooded area populated by Milwaukee brewery plutocrats and other members of the Wisconsin aristocracy who had to hire people just to count their money for them. Consequently, Hickory Hills Elementary was an elite establishment, employing two teachers for every kid. While most of the alumni would eventually go on to become world-class polo players and yachtsmen, the school wanted to reflect a more all-American image by dabbling in the mundane sport of softball.

Our ancient yellow school bus creaked under the strain of a full cargo of kids as we rode over to the Falcons' home field on Saturday. Every kid had studiously avoided sitting near me on the bus until Cora finally flopped down in the seat next to me. "Us right fielders gotta stick together," she said unceremoniously.

The oily, blue exhaust from our bus drifted over the immaculately landscaped shrubbery and bright flowers as we labored up the curved concrete driveway of Hickory Hills Elementary. The school was a campus of stately, ivy-covered brick buildings surrounded by a tall, wrought-iron riff-raff-proof fence.

At the back of the property was the softball field. The manicured grass was bracketed by two sparkling-white, machine-made foul lines emanating from home plate. Major-league style bases were firmly anchored into the ground. A large, chain-link backstop stood guard behind home plate. Bleacher seats, painted a fresh forest green, rose up along each foul line. It was a major-league ball park in miniature.

This was the *big* game of the Packawaunee Pony League. The Badgers were undefeated with a 4-0 record—leading the league—but we shared that lead with the Falcons, who were also 4-0. Even though both teams had two games remaining after this one, everyone knew that the winner of this game was certain to take the championship.

We solemnly filed off the bus, gazing with awe at the Falcons' team as they warmed up on the field. Their crisp white and navy uniforms had real numbers on the backs.

Coach Peeples held a quick meeting to go over changes in the batting lineup. I was now batting ninth, behind the two girls—the ultimate insult.

The bleachers filled up quickly with kids and parents, becoming a lively, noisy crowd with plenty of rooters for both teams. Homer Flug arrived in his pickup truck and sat with Cora.

We may have looked like hayseed cousins in our mismatched T-shirts, blue jeans, and baseball caps, but the Badgers quickly drew Falcon blood. With one runner on base, Blunt lifted a towering shot which sailed over the freshly painted Falcon fence for a home run. We led 2-0. But the Falcons struck back in the bottom of the first and tied the score.

Back and forth it went. Inning after inning I trudged out to right field and stood there like a lump while the Falcons were at bat. Inning after inning I trudged back and sat by myself on one end of the Badger bench. Every other inning or so, Peeples told me to grab a bat, whereupon I would go up to home plate and add another notch to my strikeout record.

It was probably late in the game because the sun was getting low and hitting me directly in the eyes as I stood in right field. The Hickory Hills kids in the bleachers were yelling and screaming about something, but they had been doing that on and off during the entire game. I was daydreaming in the warm sun, head down in my characteristic right-field funk. What inning is it? I wondered.

"BACK! BACK! BACK!" the center fielder screamed.

My head snapped up. The center fielder was racing over toward me. Was he yelling at *me*? Falcon runners were scurrying around the bases. The kids in the bleachers were jumping up and down. Everyone was looking in my direction. Then it dawned on me—the unthinkable had occurred.

Somebody had hit the ball into right field!

I was panic-stricken. My eyes flitted around but couldn't find the ball.

"BACK! BACK! BACK!" the center fielder screamed again.

I broke into a staggering lope toward the outfield fence, looking frantically around in the sky. The ball wasn't there.

They must be playing a joke on me—there wasn't any ball up there—nobody hits the ball to right field. But I couldn't be sure. The bright sun was blinding me—I put my glove up to shade my eyes as I staggered drunkenly toward the fence.

KA-THUNK!

My left hand was jolted by the impact. I looked at my gloved hand. The ball had come right out of the sun and nestled neatly into the webbing of my glove.

The center fielder rushed up and jumped on my back, knocking me to the grass. "Ya saved th'game! Ya saved th'game!"

Everyone was waiting for me at the Badger bench when I got in from right field. After being totally ignored just minutes before, I was now the center of attention. Kids slapped me on the back and shook my hand, exclaiming things like, *Great catch!* and *Way to go!*

I found out it had been the bottom of the seventh and final inning, and we were ahead by one run. But with two out, the Falcons had runners on second and third, with their best hitter at the plate. He promptly belted the long shot to right field that buried itself in my glove. We won the game, eleven to ten. *I was a hero.*

"I knew you had the right stuff the minute I saw you on your first day at school," Peeples said smugly as he handed me the game ball I had caught, for a keepsake. "In your case, it took a while for it to come out, but I can always spot talent."

I nodded modestly. "Yeah, Coach. I gotta admit I get off to a slow start every spring. I don't usually hit my stride until summer."

"When did you learn to catch like that?" Gertrude wanted to know.

I carefully explained to her that while it was a tricky catch in that the ball was directly in the sun, I employed a maneuver which I had devised for just that very situation. "If you get a chance like that, Gert," I advised, "just pretend you're catching the sun, and you'll make the play every time."

Homer Flug came up to me, eyes shining. "I knew that if I came to these games long enough I'd see a ball hit out to right field. I only wish it'd happened to me."

Lucky that you weren't the one out there today, Homer, I thought. You just don't have the hands.

By the time we piled back on the bus, my back was blistered from congratulatory slapping. As I walked down the aisle of the bus, Heinrich Blunt's ugly face went into some grotesque contortions which, for him, passed for a friendly grin. Gertrude smiled and gave me a flirtatious wink, completely unnerving me for a moment. Irene motioned to the empty seat next to her.

I hesitated for a moment, but then nodded respectfully to her and went to the back of the bus and sat down next to Cora.

"Us right fielders gotta stick together," I said unceremoniously.

The Education of a Damyankee

My old man had warned me that living in Hot Springs, Arkansas, was going to be different from Michigan. It was more than different—it was *weird*. For example, everybody had a telescoping metal cup that collapsed to the size of a snuff can for carrying around in their pocket. What did they use it for? *Drinking hot water.* That's right—*hot* water. The old man had bought his metal cup at the Greyhound Bus Depot when we pulled into town.

October 1945—the old man and my mother had been working at a private country club in Milwaukee, but when the golf course closed for the season, it left them out of a job. The old man, having gotten religion on natural medicine at the age of fifty, wanted to go to Hot Springs for the winter to see if the mineral water would cure his arthritis. The thought of escaping a Midwestern winter appealed to my mother, and she went along with the idea. At the age of twelve I didn't get a vote.

The first Sunday afternoon in town, we were at a public hot-water fountain in the center of Hot Springs where you could have all the free mineral water you could drink. The old man had dragged me from our rented apartment to this fountain and sweet-talked me into trying the sulphurous concoction. He pushed the steaming cup into my hand. "It ain't s'bad if ya drink it fast."

I pinched my nose, closed my eyes, and gulped it down. He lied—it was awful. The city advertised that the hot mineral water occurred naturally, deep in the ground, but I figured a bunch of ex-moonshiners in the hills secretly brewed the water and trucked it into town in the middle of the night. Nothing that tasted that bad could occur naturally.

"Ya keep drinkin' th'water here, an' you'll live t'be a hunnert years old," the old man claimed.

Hah! If you drank this stuff every day, it would only *seem* like a hundred years.

Looking at all the white faces at the fountain, I asked the old man, "If this water is so good, why don't the colored people come down here and drink it?"

He paused. "They got their own fountain."

I didn't know it at the time, but this was my introduction to segregation.

The next day I started school in the seventh grade at Hot Springs Central Junior High. At the beginning of the first period, I stood in the back of the homeroom until the teacher walked in and rapped on her desk with the blackboard pointer. "Lissinup, yawl. Ah'd lahk t'welcum a new boy from th'nawth. His nayum's Gerawld." She pointed at me.

That was another thing about Hot Springs. It was in the United States, but they spoke a foreign language.

At the end of the period, I lugged an armload of books up to my assigned hallway locker. While I was struggling to get the key in the lock, someone tried to rearrange my vertebrae with a hard bodycheck from behind, knocking the books to the floor. I swung around and faced a gigantic red-haired kid with mean green eyes sticking a key in my locker. He was about twice my size, so I just meekly picked up the books. They had told me at the principal's office that I would be sharing a locker with some other kid.

"Are you B. D. Purvis?" I ventured.

"Yup."

"I'm your new locker-mate."

"Not fer lawng y'ain't. Ain't gohna cozy up t'no damyankee. Gohna git me 'nuther lahcker."

I hung on every word he said. I'd discovered during first period that they were speaking *English*, but you had to listen very carefully. I didn't pick up everything he said, but B. D., whatever that stood for, didn't sound like he wanted to become a close pal of mine.

"Pop, what's a damyankee?"
The old man looked up from his newspaper. "Where'd ya hear that?"
"School. That's what my locker-mate called me."
The old man barked out a laugh.
"Ain't funny. He won't talk to me. He acts like I'm some kind'a freak."
"A damyankee—tha's what some southerners, th'ones still fightin' th'Civil War, call people from the north."
"Why? The Civil War was eighty years ago. His *grandfather* wasn't even born then."
"Yeah . . . well . . . give 'im a li'l time. He'll come 'round once he gets used to ya."

But that never happened. I did all right in school, and the teachers treated me okay, but as the weeks inched by into November, I was still a damyankee to B. D. Purvis. He wasn't able to switch his locker, and that must have really made him mad because he quit talking to me altogether. That was okay with me, but he had somehow convinced the other kids that a damyankee was no one they wanted to associate with.

So I ate lunch by myself, read books in the homeroom during recess, and took in a lot of movies alone in the evenings and on weekends. I drank the hot water, but it didn't make me feel any better. I hated Hot Springs and counted the days until we would go north in the spring.

One day I took my new football to school, hoping that somebody might want to throw it around with me. Touch football was a hot pastime, and B. D. and his cronies always had a game in the schoolyard at recess but never included me. At recess I stood alone next to the chain-link fence with the ball under my arm.

"Wanna toss th'bawl 'round?"

A tall, gangly kid I hadn't noticed before was talking to me. He looked like he had just jumped out of the Li'l Abner comic strip—an ugly-looking sucker—dark, rotten front teeth—long, scraggly black hair—patched, faded overalls and a plaid shirt. So what, at least he was talking.

"Sure," I said eagerly, flipping him the football. He took the ball and faded back about thirty yards. *Where's he going? Did Purvis send him over to steal my football?* He cocked his arm and threw the ball.

It ripped toward me like a fat, brown rifle slug, tightly spiralling as it hummed through the air. The football slammed into my chest, almost impaling me on the chain-link fence.

"Sawrry," he said.

I scrabbled after the ball, picked it up, and ran over to him. I couldn't throw a football half that far, and I sure didn't want him firing it back at me. "Kin you show me how t'throw like that?" I blurted.

"Lahk whut?"

"Make the ball spiral."

He grinned. "Shore cahyan. Et's eahzy t'do." The words oozed out of his mouth like maple syrup. He held out his hand. "Ah'm Roy Watkins." He added with a lazy wink, "Ah'll even show yew how t'*ketch* it."

The rest of the week Roy and I threw the football during recess. He showed me how to hold the ball—fingertips on the laces—push it out and let it roll off the fingers as you throw it. With Roy's coaching, my passes improved considerably. I also learned how to catch Roy's passes, although he'd cut way down on the velocity to keep from killing me.

Things were looking up in Hot Springs—I had a friend. After school, Roy and I would throw the football in the street outside my apartment house until dark. But it was a busy street, and the traffic kept interrupting us. One day my mother told us she didn't want us playing in that street any more and if we wanted to throw the football after school, we had to go over to Roy's house. I looked at Roy, but he shook his head with a strange look on his face. For some reason he didn't want me at his house.

"Thayat figgers." Those were the first words that Purvis had spoken to me in weeks. We were getting our books out of the locker before the first-period classes.

"What?"

"Thayat a damyankee'd pal 'round with wahte trash."

"What's wahte trash?" I asked.

Purvis gave me a violent shove into the locker door. "Yew mahkin' fun a me, boy? Ah'm tawkin' 'bout yew an' thayat Watkins playin' patty cayak with th'footbawl et recess."

"What's wrong with that? Nobody else even talks t'me."

"Don' yew know nuthin? He lives in *niggahtown.* He's wahte trash."

I grabbed my books and went off down the hall, deep in thought. In the weeks that I had been in Hot Springs, I'd seen plenty of black people but only in the streets downtown. There weren't any in the neighborhood where we lived. There weren't any at Hot Springs Central Junior High. There weren't any at the church where we went on Sunday morning. I saw them at the same movie theaters that I went to, but they had a separate door and went up to the balcony while I had to sit on the first floor. Too bad—I preferred balconies when I went to the show. They had separate drinking fountains. I wanted to try their water because it certainly couldn't be any worse than the stuff the white people were drinking. My old man told me to forget it.

I was fascinated—after you left downtown Hot Springs, the black people faded into thin air. Where did they go? I wanted to see where they lived.

As usual, Roy and I threw the football at recess. "Hey, let's throw the ball over at your house this Saturday," I suggested.

Roy looked uneasy. "Ah . . . nah . . . et's purty far from here, an' . . . an' ah got sum other thangs t'do Saturday."

I held on to the football and walked over to him. "C'mon . . . Purvis tol' me where you live . . . it's okay."

His face fell. "Et's only fur a li'l while . . . we'ull be movin' purty soon. Mah place shore ain' much t'look at . . . y'wouldn' lahk et."

"I wanna see it anyhow. I'll be over Saturday afternoon . . . okay?"

Roy finally agreed and must have gotten comfortable with it because he invited me for Saturday lunch.

When I trudged out on the far end of Center Street on Saturday morning, I was in unfamiliar territory. I left behind the brick apartment buildings and the stately Southern homes. Now the houses were small, wood frame, and badly in need of paint.

As I got close to Roy's place, the streets became crooked dirt roads with only an occasional 1930's vintage car to be seen. Tall eucalyptus and magnolia trees arched over the roads. Almost every house had large, fragrant flowering bushes around the walls to cover up the peeling paint. It reminded me a lot of south Ishpeming in the Upper Peninsula of Michigan where I was brought up—old houses—big trees—quiet and rural—except for the black faces staring at me as I shuffled through the dust with the football under my arm.

Roy's house was a small, square bungalow with a sagging front porch. A crack in one of the front windows had been patched with white adhesive tape. I knocked on the door, and Roy opened it immediately, like he had been waiting behind it for me to arrive.

The house had three small rooms. The main room was crowded with a cast-iron wood stove, sink, wooden icebox, oilcloth-covered table with four mismatched chairs, and an ancient, faded couch. Two unpainted, old wooden crates had been nailed to the wall over the sink for cupboards. The other two rooms were small bedrooms. No bathroom—a privy outside. Wooden plank floors—clean, but no rugs.

A thin, pale woman with her hair tied up in a red bandanna wiped her hands on her apron and gave me a shy smile. "Ah'm Roy's mama." She pulled out one of the chairs. "Siddown, won'cha. We'ah fixin' t'eat. His paw ain't here . . . got a day job on thayat new road nawth a town."

Roy and I sat down at the table, and his mother brought two pans over from the stove. She speared wieners out of one pan—two for each of us—then spooned out some white stuff from the other, putting a big glob of it on my plate. Bringing a metal pitcher from the sink, she filled up jelly-jar glasses with lukewarm lemonade—motioning with her head toward the ice-box. "Ain't got no ice t'day. Mebbe nex' week."

She sat down. I started to reach for the glass of lemonade, but both of them bowed their heads and clasped their hands. I was caught off guard—my parents never said grace at the table—my mother reasoning that bedtime and Sundays were when Lutherans prayed. In a quiet, clear voice, Roy's mother spoke a few words, thanking the Lord for the bountiful meal we were about to receive.

Roy excitedly grabbed a piece of white bread from an open loaf in the center of the table. "Saturday's hot dawg day." He quickly wrapped the bread around a wiener and poured on catsup.

I followed his lead, but when he poured catsup on the glop of white stuff on his plate, I stopped. "Is this Cream of Wheat?" I asked.

His mother smiled politely. "No, honey, et's grits."

"Grits?"

"Roy sez yawl from up nawth. Mebbe y'don' git grits up thayre. Usually y'put buttah on et, but we don' have buttah t'day so y'miaht try th'ketchup."

I tried the grits with catsup. It wasn't bad, but of course, catsup was my favorite food.

Roy's mother gazed around the room and sighed. "Hope t'move inta a bettah place when Roy's paw finds steady work. Got t'git outta this neigh-borhood."

"It's nice here," I said, chewing a mouthful of white-bread hot dog. "Kind'a like where we used to live in Upper Michigan."

That got her attention. "Yew live with colored folks up thayah?"

"No . . . never seen none there . . . I meant the houses, big trees, dirt roads . . . things like that. This's the best part of Hot Springs. If we lived down here all the time, this's where I'd wanna live. Right here on this street."

"Ah don' thank yew would. We'ah th'only wahte people on this street."

"Izzat bad?" I asked.

She stared at me hard for a few moments. In a lighter voice she said, "Ah guess it ain' s'bad. Lots'a nice folks 'roun' here." She stood up suddenly. "You kids want 'nother wiener? Ah thank thayre's two left."

Roy leaned over to me and said in a whisper. "She mus' *lahke* yew. She *nevah* offers me th'extra wieners."

After our hot dog, grits, and lemonade lunch, Roy and I went outside with my football. Standing on his front porch, Roy yelled at the house next door. "Hey, Dawg! C'mon out fer sum footbawl!"

Next door a tall black kid opened the battered screen door and slowly stepped out on his porch. All he had on was a pair of bib overalls—no shirt or shoes. He stood there looking me over suspiciously.

"This here's a pal a mahn frum school . . . nayum's Jerry," Roy said, tossing my football to Dawg.

Dawg's eyes widened when he got a good look at the new football. "Gollamighty, Roy, wher'ja git this bawl?" He spun it up in the air and caught it a few times to get the feel of it. "Le's git Smoke an' have a gayum a touch."

The three of us went across the road and Dawg yelled at a gray house. "Smoke! Footbawl!"

A small, sinewy black kid came out. He wore thick, wire-rimmed glasses that made his eyes look huge. He carried a football, but it had definitely seen better days. The seams were coming loose on the ends, and it was scuffed beyond belief. In his other hand he held a bicycle pump.

"Ol' bawl leaks," Roy said to me. "Hafta keep pumpin' et up ever' coupl'a minutes." Then to Smoke, "Leave th'ol bawl home . . . we got us a new one."

Smoke walked slowly over to my ball in Dawg's hand. He poked it lightly with a finger and then squeezed it hard with his hand. "Don' hafta pump et up?"

"Nope," Roy said. "B'longs to mah pal Jerry, here."

Smoke took his eyes off the football and looked up at me solemnly. "Yawl mus' be rich t'own a bawl lahk thayat."

It was glorious—a whole afternoon of touch football. We played right in the middle of the dirt road, which we had all to ourselves since no one around there had cars to drive. The road—Sledgehammer Alley—got its name because so many of the men living there had day jobs doing road work on the local streets and highways.

I spent the following two Saturday afternoons over there. Dawg and Smoke were shy at first, only accepting me because I was Roy's friend and it was *my* football, but I quickly became just one of the gang. After the games we would build a fire at the edge of Sledgehammer Alley and roast potatoes. I had never tasted a potato roasted over an open fire—it was good.

One Monday in late November, Roy and I went to my locker at recess to get the football. It wasn't there.

"Purvis took it," I snapped. "I know I put it in there before first period this morning."

"Why wud he do that? Thay already got a bawl thay use et recess."

"I dunno. Let's go find him."

Sure enough, B. D. Purvis and his gang were using my football in the schoolyard. I was really steamed and without thinking, charged right into the middle of their game. "That's my football."

Before he said a word, Purvis shoved me to the ground. "Git outta here yankee . . . cain't yew see we got a gayum goin'?"

"You took my football out of the locker."

Purvis smirked. "Wut mahkes yew an expert on footbawls? They awl look alahk."

I stared at the ball under his arm. I had put my name on it with a fountain pen. Purvis had tried to rub it out, but the ink smudges still were on the ball. He intended to keep it. I jabbed a finger at the smudges. "That's where my name was."

Purvis' face went cold and mean. He jerked his head toward Roy. "Mebbe yew and this wahte trash'd lahk to fight us for thayat bawl."

Roy made a strange sound in his throat, turned red, and went as stiff as a board. After a moment he spoke in a quiet, flat voice I had never heard before. "Too many a yew t'take on, but we'ull play yew fer th'bawl."

"Whut?" Purvis said.

"Saturday aft'noon. We'ull have a gayum. Winnah keeps th'bawl."

"Hah! Whut . . . yew two agin' us?"

"We'ull git two more . . . agin yew'n three others," Roy said.

"We'ud whup yewr ahss." Purvis snapped. "'Sides, we already got th'bawl. Don' haft'a play no gayum fer et."

"If we lose, I'll clean all my stuff out'a the locker," I said. "You kin have it all to yourself."

Silence. A group of kids had gathered around, listening to the exchange. "Take 'em on, B. D.," somebody yelled.

"Lahcker to m'self, huh? Okay," Purvis said with a crafty smile and then a nod. "Saturday aft'noon . . . raht here in the yard."

"No," Roy said. "Over to mah place. Th'other two cain't play in this schoolyard."

Purvis's eyes bugged out. "Th'uther two're niggahs? Yew want us to play footbawl agin *niggahs*? Et figgers. Who else'd yew b'able to git fer yer team?"

"Course, if yew figger y'myaht git beat . . . " Roy said.

All eyes looked at Purvis. "We'ull be thayre," he said.

After school I went over to Sledgehammer Alley with Roy to break the news of Saturday's game to Dawg and Smoke.

We sat on the steps of Dawg's front porch, Dawg pulling absently at loose tatters on the cuffs of his overalls. "Ah don' wanna play footbawl again' wahte boys. Thay myaht lynch us if we win."

"Thay myaht lynch us if we *lose*," Smoke said bleakly.

"Don't be dumb," I said. "This is 1945. They don't do things like that anymore."

"Whudda yew know 'bout lynchin' . . . livin' up thayre in Eskimo lan'?" Dawg said.

"Ain' nobody gonna git lynched," Roy said firmly. "Game's gonna be raht here on this road . . . everbody's gonna be watchin'. We gotta play 'em t'git th'bawl back. An' 'sides . . . ah gotta score t'settle with Purvis."

"How big are these wahte boys?" Smoke asked.

"Bigger'n us," Roy said. "But big ain' alwayahs best."

Saturday afternoon at two o'clock, the four of them came. Long before we could see them we could see the large cloud of dust in their wake. Purvis, carrying my football, had brought his three most-feared sidekicks.

Stonewall Munk—sharp, deep-set, predator eyes. To him, touch football meant taking a bite out of the ball carrier's arm.

Razorback Mudd—spikey hair jutting up all over his skull—raw power, speed, and nastiness—his favorite trick on defense was boxing the ears of the opposition, shaping their heads into long, thin wedges.

Bubba Pew—I had yet to hear Bubba utter any sound that could be classified as human speech. Rhinoceros-like eyes, one on each side of his head—Bubba was in the same weight class as the USS *Missouri*. His job was running interference for the guy carrying the football. By the time you circled around Bubba, you were badly winded and the ball carrier was in the end zone with the ball.

They ground to a halt at Roy's porch where we were waiting. All four of them wearing splendidly white T-shirts with the Confederate flag sewn on the front. A lightning bolt was hand-stitched over the flag. The shirts had probably been made specially for this game. "We'ah th'Lightnin' Rebels," Purvis said proudly, pointing to his shirt. "Didn' know we's gonna play th'gayum in th'city dump, or we wudn't'a worn our good uniforms."

"Thay mus' be rich t'have uniforms lahk thayat," Smoke said enviously.

"How cum we don' have a team nayum?" Dawg whispered to me.

"How about 'the Damyankees?'" I replied.

"Damyankees? . . . *Us?*" Dawg asked.

"Ain' muchuva nayum," Smoke said.

"No time t'argue 'bout nayums," Roy said. Then jerking his head toward me, he added, "Et's his footbawl so he gits t'pick th'nayum. 'Damyankees' et iz."

We briefly settled on ground rules and boundaries. Touch football is much simpler than regular football—four downs to make a touchdown—no punts. A touchdown counted six points. Since there wasn't a goal post—no extra-point kicks or field goals. The defense had to touch the ball carrier with two hands on the head, torso, or legs.

The playing field was Sledgehammer Alley. The sidelines extended to the porches of the houses on both sides of the road and the end zones were the crossroads in both directions from Roy's house. We ended up with a football field one-hundred-and-fifty yards long with a dogleg to the left.

Slowly and quietly, screen doors started to open. People drifted out onto their porches to watch. No cheers or talking—just curious onlookers.

We flipped a penny to see who received the ball first. Purvis's team won. I held the ball upright on the ground with my finger and Roy kicked. A nice kick—it sailed straight down the road a long way. But Purvis caught it cleanly.

Roy and I had seen the Purvis flying wedge at the schoolyard, but Dawg and Smoke were about to get their first look at it. Stonewall, Razorback, and Bubba clustered around Purvis, who was carrying the football, and they rumbled toward our goal line in tight formation. The ground shook as they bore down on us. These guys outweighed us by a half ton, so getting to the ball carrier was like trying to shoulder your way into a stampeding herd of Longhorn cattle. I caught a straight-arm in the face from Bubba that left me sprawled in the dust.

Nobody touched Purvis, and he ran all the way for a touchdown. Chortling insanely, he yelled at me. "Yankee, ah spec' yew t'have all yewr crap outta mah lahcker by firs' period on Monday."

"We ain' th'Yankees . . . we's th'*Dam*yankees," Dawg yelled back.

Purvis gave him a puzzled look and shook his head as his team trotted back for the kickoff.

They kicked the ball—a low screamer right at me. I dropped it. Luckily, Roy fell on it before the other team could recover the fumble.

We went into a huddle—a long way from the goal line. Roy looked at Smoke, frowning. "How cum yew ain' wearin' yewr glasses?"

"M'mama wouldn' let me . . . playin' agin' big wahte boys . . . glasses cos' tew much."

"Kin yew see?" Roy asked.

"Ah kin see whare thay iz," Smoke said. "Tha's good 'nuff if yawl don' throw th'bawl at me . . . jus' han' et t'me nice'n easy."

We had decided our offensive positions beforehand: Roy, quarterback; Dawg, pass receiver; Smoke, running back; and being the lousiest player, I was the center.

Roy called the play. "Smoke . . . sweep left," he whispered.

I bent over the ball on the line of scrimmage. Bubba towered over me in his defensive crouch, snorting and pawing the ground with his knuckles.

Nervously, I grabbed the ball with both hands, looked at Roy from between my legs, and flipped it to him.

The Lightning Rebels let out ear-splitting rebel yells and charged across the line of scrimmage. Bubba mashed me flat with his telephone-pole forearm. Roy handed the ball to Smoke—Smoke stood there for a moment with the ball, looking myopically at the four monsters bearing down on him—his eyes trying to focus.

Purvis saw Smoke's hesitation, and his eyes gleamed with delight as he stormed in. He had no intention of just touching Smoke. He wanted to flatten him. Arms outstretched, he launched himself through the air at Smoke.

All Purvis got was a noseful of dirt as he sprawled to the ground. I had found out that first Saturday how Smoke got his name. He had this

Smoke stood there for a moment with the ball, looking myopically at the four monsters bearing down on him.

nasty little habit of disappearing into thin air whenever he had the ball. *He was the fastest runner I'd ever seen in my life.* Looking up from where I lay, I saw a trail of dust leading to the Lightning Rebels' goal line. Smoke was standing in the end zone with the football.

The Lightning Rebels were in shock. Open-mouthed, they couldn't believe that a runty, barefooted black boy had shown them up. Hoots and hollers with scattered hand-clapping came from the spectators on the porches.

We kicked off, but the Rebels showed us their flying wedge again. In two plays they galloped in for another touchdown. The score was Lightning Rebels—12, Damyankees—6.

We got the ball again, and on the first down Roy faded back for a pass. Dawg, covered by Razorback and Stonewall, loped down toward the Lightning Rebels' end zone. Bubba, snorting and bellowing, rushed in at Roy. At the last second, Roy side-stepped him like a matador and launched one of his bullet passes. When he had a football in his hands, Roy didn't look like a hillbilly at all. He looked more like the quarterback for the Green Bay Packers. The ball screamed toward the end zone ten feet in the air. Razorback, Stonewall, and Dawg leaped up in unison, but when it came to jumping, nobody could match Dawg. His long arms shot up three feet over Razorback's and Stonewall's fingertips. He snatched the ball with one hand. Tie game.

All afternoon the battle raged on. When the Lightning Rebels had the ball they stampeded it in for a touchdown. They were too big—we couldn't get through their flying wedge. Also, Smoke and Dawg felt intimidated by the big white kids wearing Confederate flags on their chest.

But the Lightning Rebels couldn't hold us either, with Smoke running the ball in for touchdowns and Roy firing his high hard passes to Dawg in the end zone.

Seeing that this wasn't the easy win that they though it was going to be, the Lightning Rebels were taking out their frustrations with their "touches." As far as they were concerned, this wasn't touch football anymore. Whenever they were able to reach Smoke carrying the ball, they sent him flying, ass over teakettle. Dawg got even worse treatment. He would leap up to catch a pass and get upended in mid air, often landing on his head. Smoke was limping badly, and Dawg had a very sore neck. It was only a matter of time before we caved in.

But the other team didn't look too good either. Their once-proud T-shirts were caked with dirt and sweat, and the lightning bolts hung limply from broken threads. They were used to playing only half-hour recess games, and we had been going at it for three hours. Their tongues were hanging out, and Bubba's face was beet red.

The sun was low when Smoke's father yelled a two-minute warning from the porch. "Suppah in two minutes!"

Smoke shook his head in resignation. "He mean bus'ness. He don' never yell twice. Ah don' cum in . . . he cum an' gits me. Thayat's et fer th'gayum, ah guess."

This was bad. The score was tied at sixty, but they had the ball. If they scored another touchdown, we wouldn't even have time to try to score again.

"Lissin," Roy said quickly. "We gotta git 'em t'fumble th'bawl. Smoke, yew git en thare through thayat wedge an' knock et outta Purvis' han's."

Smoke looked at Roy in horror. "He gonna kill me if ah do thayat."

"He'ull be too busy tryin' t'git th'bawl back. Yew *gotta* do et. Yewr th'only one who's fas' 'nough." Roy stared at Smoke intently for a few long seconds. Smoke finally nodded.

The Lightning Rebels broke out of their huddle, confident smirks on their dusty faces—victory within their grasp. "This iz et, yankee," Purvis rasped at me. "We're gonna draw las' blood."

At that moment a county dump truck loaded down with men and road-working equipment came rattling down the road and stopped by Roy's house. A white man who looked a lot like Roy got off, stood there in his tar-splattered shirt for a few seconds staring at the Lightning Rebels, and then went into Roy's house.

The truck was blocking part of the road, but the Lightning Rebels were intent on getting their game-winning touchdown. They quickly went into their flying wedge and swept to the right—Purvis carrying the ball as usual. Smoke circled around their right flank, but Bubba, lumbering along, kept a wary eye on him, hands ready to push him off. With a terrific burst of speed Smoke headed right for Bubba and the center of the wedge.

Bubba was surprised—neither one of the black kids had made a move like that all afternoon. He reached out to grab Smoke, but Smoke scrunched down to a foot off the ground, slithering under Bubba's grasp. With surgical precision, Smoke went after the football under Purvis' right arm. He popped it loose with a tiny fist.

A mad scramble—the ball bounced off somebody's hands and sailed high into the air. Everybody jumped for it, and the ball bounced again and again off heads and hands—higher and higher. In one last graceful arc, the football plopped into the bed of the dump truck. The truck driver, unaware of this, put the truck into gear and pulled away.

For a long moment, the eight of us stood there and watched the truck disappearing down the road. No one could think of anything to say. Then Dawg wandered off—Smoke hurried home to get his supper.

The Lightning Rebels started to leave. Purvis paused by Roy and me, his face streaked with sweat and dust. He gave us a tired but respectful nod. "See yawl Monday, ah guess. We'ull have a gayum goin' in th'yard at recess. Ah . . . yewr welcum t'play if'n yew want." Then he added, "Too bad them uther two ain' wahte. Ah shore cud use them, too."

It was a warm March morning, and the old man was checking our footlockers in with the bus driver at the Hot Springs' Greyhound Bus depot. My mother stood nearby, poised with an A&P shopping bag full of roast-beef sandwiches for the long trip north.

Roy, Smoke, and Dawg had come down to see me off, even wearing shoes for the occasion. We stood around for a few minutes, not knowing what to say or do. I never thought I'd be reluctant to leave Hot Springs, but I was having trouble swallowing the lump in my throat.

"Lookit thayat big bus," Smoke said. "Yawl mus' be rich t'ride inna bus lahk thayat."

"Y'cummin' back?" Dawg asked.

"Don't know," I said. "Good luck if you play the Lightnin' Rebels again."

"Don' thank so," Dawg said. "Wahte an' colored prob'ly *nevah* play football t'gethah . . . sumbody git killed."

"All 'board!" the bus driver called.

I moved toward the bus. "Look . . . there's a good window seat in the back."

"Ain' yawl learn nuthin' here?" Smoke said scornfully. "On'y colored gits t'ride en th'back. Yew ride en front whare yawl b'long."

"Yeah, I forgot."

I waved at them and got on the bus. There was only an aisle seat in the front. The old man had told me that by dark we would be in Illinois—the north. I hoped that by then that window seat in the back of the bus would still be empty.

The Catechism Scam

"Omygawdtheministerscoming," my mother gasped from the kitchen window. She had this habit of keeping an eye on our front path since people in our little town in the Upper Michigan woods were inclined to drop in anytime on unannounced visits. This morning her vigilance paid off—we had thirty seconds' warning—the time it would take Pastor Karppi to walk from our front gate to the kitchen door.

My old man, in frayed long underwear, was settled into his usual early-morning slouch at the kitchen table. His false teeth sat fizzing in a jelly-jar glass of dental cleaner on the table. He had a saucer of coffee halfway to his mouth and froze like a deer caught in the headlights. "Why th'hell's he cummin here now? We been goin' t'church regular."

My mother didn't answer—she was already in frenzied motion—weaving and bobbing like a Thai kick boxer. With one hand, she yanked off her apron and house dress in a single motion. With the other, she jerked open the oven door, chucking in the ever-present plate of bear claws and sliced pound cake to warm. She kicked off her bedroom slippers, sailing them neatly into the pantry. "Quit swearing and get dressed," she yelled at the old man as she dashed into the bedroom.

"What'll I put on?" he asked, running after her.

"Your good pants and that new shirt that just came from Sears. And put your teeth in!"

I tore into my bedroom, scrambling out of my overalls and into my church-going pants. I doused my cowlick with a generous glug of Wildroot Creme Oil and plastered it down with the comb.

Lutheranism, as practiced in the 1940's rural Midwest, was a raw, no-nonsense business. A church member was expected to attend regularly and for life. If you missed too many Sundays, the minister came looking for you. He would inquire politely about your health, but he was really checking the dipstick of your moral fortitude.

A knock rattled the kitchen door. With amazing athletic ability, my mother bounded out of the bedroom, crossed the kitchen floor in two leaps, and opened the door with a broad, beaming smile. "Oh, Pastor Karppi, what a pleasant surprise," she said in a breathless voice. "Come in . . . we were just sitting down to coffee."

In under half a minute, this severe-looking Finnish housewife in a dowdy Gold Medal flour-sack dress with a dust kerchief on her head had become a remarkable likeness of Katherine Hepburn. She had on her dark-blue wool church-going dress with matching shoes—a touch of lipstick—a faint blush of rouge—every hair in place—the same woman who took an hour and a half to get ready for church.

The old man lurched out of the bedroom buttoning his shirt cuffs. He had inadvertently managed a very stiff and pious appearance by forgetting to take the cardboard out of the collar of the new shirt he was wearing.

Pastor Karppi came in and was ushered into the living room. Our one good living room chair, the old man's leather, over-stuffed easy chair, was immediately given over to the minister. *The Mining Journal* sports page, which had been lying on the heavy oak library table just moments before, had magically metamorphosed into a Holy Bible.

My mother quickly dealt with the essential preliminaries of putting cups and saucers, plates, silverware, napkins, and the warm pastries on the library table. Three kitchen chairs were dragged into the living room. She poured three coffees and mixed an Ovaltine for me. I had been drinking coffee for a year, but apparently my hard-earned coffee privilege had been cancelled for the duration of the minister's visit.

Precariously balancing cups and saucers and pastry plates on pressed-together knees, the three of us nervously waited for words of Lutheran wisdom to roll out of Pastor Karppi's mouth. Karppi only heightened our anxiety while he methodically slathered butter on a thick slice of warm pound cake. Then he ate slowly, his jowls flapping in rhythm with each chew.

The minister was on the plump side—an occupational hazard of consuming pastries during his many unannounced forays into the congregation's households. However, ice-blue eyes glinting between folds of fat were indicators of the real Karppi personality. It was well known that those eyes could bore right into your soul, ferreting out un-Lutheran-like thoughts and deeds with such speed and precision that your only recourse was to fall on the floor, sobbing out confessions.

Only after finishing his second slice of pound cake did Pastor Karppi clear his throat. "This is not really a social visit," he stated, casually brushing cake crumbs from his shiny black trousers. "I have come on church business."

Usually, when a minister made an opening statement like that, it was going to cost money. Forgetting that she was no longer wearing an apron, my mother began to wipe her hands apprehensively on the front of her good dress.

"As you know . . . your son," he nodded his head toward me, "is coming of age for confirmation into the Bethany Lutheran Church. I am starting preparatory classes two weeks from Saturday. I expect that you will want him to attend."

She breathed an audible sigh of relief. "Of course, Pastor. He'll be there."

"I will be schooling the boys and girls quite thoroughly every Saturday morning for three months . . . "

I put down my bear claw. *Wait a minute—every Saturday morning for three months?* My Saturdays were all taken up with top-priority projects—building model airplanes—killing rats at the town dump—going over to the pool hall to swap romantic-conquest lies with my pals.

I didn't even know what confirmation was. My mother kept threatening that it was going to happen to me someday, but I had filed it away with the three other unavoidable future unpleasantries—college, marriage, and death.

Karppi reached into a jacket pocket, brought out a small book, and handed it to me. "This is a gift from the church, young man. You would profit by starting to read it before our first Saturday session. The contents must be memorized by the time we have our confirmation service."

I looked at the book cover. *A Short Explanation of Dr. Martin Luther's Small Catechism.* I'd be lucky if I memorized the title.

The following Monday, Carl Kettu and I were over at Chub Mattila's Standard Station, indulging in our usual lunch-hour refuge from the oppressive atmosphere of school. Carl sat hunched over on the soda pop cooler next to the cash register, eyes riveted on the latest "eight-pager" in Chub's collection. "Eight-pagers" were pocket-sized, sexually explicit comic books ground out in the wee hours on basement presses far to the south of us in Chicago or Milwaukee. Chub bought them from northbound truckers and let us look at them free of charge. He knew that smutty pictures made us young studs very thirsty, and he figured as long as we were going to hang around his station, he might as well make some money on soda pop sales.

The size of the "eight-pager" brought the catechism to mind. "Did Karppi bring a catechism to yer house?" I asked Carl.

Carl didn't answer. He was in a deep pornographic trance, memorizing every detail of the exaggerated female anatomies. I jabbed him. "Whut?" he mumbled, sucking on his Nesbitt's Orange soda pop, not looking up. I repeated the question. He finally took his eyes off the book and glared at me, not believing I had the sheer effrontery to bring up a subject so joltingly far removed from his current passion. "Yeah, he did. Whaddabout it?"

"Didja look at it? It's full of questions and answers. It's like a test."

"Izzat right?" Carl went back to the "eight-pager."

"Karppi sez we gotta learn all the answers before confirmation. That's a lotta work."

Carl snickered. "That's what's botherin' you? Ferget it . . . all that happens at confirmation is ya dress up in stupid gowns, get up in front of the church congregation, the minister makes a speech, sez a few prayers, everybody sings 'A Mighty Fortress Is Our God,' an' that's it. My older brother went through it three years ago, an' he didn't study no catechism."

"Yeah, but that was when old Rinnemaki was the minister. I dunno . . . I think Karppi's different."

"All them ministers are the same," Carl said with finality, sticking his nose back in the book.

All ministers were *not* the same. Pastor Karppi made that very clear at our first Saturday-morning preparatory class. Fourteen pimply faced adolescents were assembled around a long wooden table in the basement of the Lutheran church. Sitting at the head of the table with his hands folded, Karppi opened the session by addressing Carl Kettu. "Carl, how many kinds of sin are there?"

Carl, staring at a wall picture of "The Last Supper," wrestled with the question for several seconds. "Twelve?" he ventured, thinking that perhaps each disciple had been in charge of a particular category of sin.

It sounded like a fair estimate to me, but Karppi glared at Carl, slowly shook his head, and turned to one of the girls. "Martha, do you know the answer?"

Martha Paksu—a plump bookworm with thick glasses, recognized as our class intellectual—fired it out with machine-gun rapidity. "There are two kinds of sin: original sin and actual sin.'"

Karppi nodded. "That's right. Reino, can you tell me what original sin is?"

Reino Rovaneimi looked at the ceiling while he conjured up an answer. "Well . . . original sin . . . is . . . when ya do somethin' bad that nobody else ever thought of doin' before."

I was sure that Reino had hit it right on the nose, and it even drew some appreciative chuckles from the boys, but Karppi didn't like that answer at all. He slammed his open hand down on the table with such force that catechisms all down the line flipped up in the air.

He began speaking with a menacing quietness. "I can see that you boys think that this is some sort of frivolous activity not worthy of your time and effort. I brought catechisms to all of your homes weeks ago, and apparently, little has been done with them." He paused and leaned forward, his voice rising. "Do you know what the confirmation process is? *It's an oral examination!* I will be asking you questions out of the catechism and you will give the answers in front of the whole congregation. Your family . . . your friends . . . every Lutheran in town will be there!" He got up from his seat and walked slowly around the table. "And do you know what will happen if you don't give the answers to my satisfaction? *You will not be confirmed!*"

Realizing that he was starting to shout, Karppi got a grip on himself. "But I'm a reasonable man," he said, calming down. "If you fail, I will let you try again. Of course, you will have to attend this preparatory class every Saturday until we have another confirmation ceremony . . . many months later . . . and if you fail again, there's always a third time . . . and a fourth." He smiled grimly and picked up a catechism from the table and began tapping it with his finger. "So you see . . . either you get this material . . . ," his voice started to rise again, " . . . or I get *you!*" For added emphasis, he jabbed his finger at Reino's face, bringing it to a halt within an inch of his nose. Reino turned the color of Cream of Wheat, melted into a quivering blob, and started to slide off his chair.

Karppi marched back to his chair and sat down. "Now boys, let's start on something much simpler . . . something *everybody* knows . . . so these girls won't think you're total idiots." He looked at me. "Gerald, tell us how many Commandments there are."

> *He's talking to me! Wait a minute . . . the Commandments . . . this is easy . . . we went over this in Sunday School plenty of times. It's eight . . . no . . . it's twelve . . . or was it six?*

Karppi kept looking at me with that icy stare.

During the following week, I took the catechism and really whipped my brain into a gallop. I memorized all Ten Commandments and could discourse knowledgeably on the meaning of each one. I painstakingly dissected and digested the Apostle's Creed, article by article. I could even give you the precise definition and function of angels.

On Saturday I went to the second preparatory class, my head bulging with Lutheran miscellany. But as soon as Pastor Karppi asked me a question and drilled me with *those eyes*, my memory was wiped clean as a Monday-morning blackboard.

I wasn't the only one. One look from Karppi, and Reino couldn't even remember the English language. Carl wasn't much better. Even the girls, who were known experts in religious lore, sputtered when Karppi quizzed them. And it didn't improve in the weeks to follow. Studying was futile when your teacher had this evil eye that instantly sucked every drop of knowledge out of your skull. If we were *ever* going to get out of these Saturday sweatsessions in the Lutheran church basement, something had to be done.

"I've got it! I've got it!" Carl cried, rushing into Chub's station one Friday night where Reino and I were drowning our sorrows in soda pop. "I know how we're gonna get confirmed."

Our faces hardened with suspicion. Carl was notorious for masterminding sure-fire schemes that usually buckled under their own weight, with us underneath. "How we gonna do that?" I asked.

Carl produced a photograph. It was a confirmation picture taken in front of the altar of the Bethany Lutheran Church. Pastor Rinnemaki and a group of kids in long gowns stared solemnly into the camera. I knew them all. It was the confirmation class from three years ago with Carl's older brother, Melvin.

"So what?" Reino said.

"Lookit them gowns," Carl said. "Those big sleeves reach all the way to the fingertips. You could hide a catechism easy in your hand."

Reino sneered at him scornfully. "So whatcha gonna do? Karppi asks you a question, an' you say, 'Just a minute,' while you page through the book in front of everybody lookin' for the answer?"

Carl chuckled at Reino's lack of acuity. "Look at the picture again," he said patiently. Since they're taller, the guys are standin' in the back row. All ya kin see is their shoulders and heads. Ya just stand there with the book down in your hands. When he asks you a question ya jus' bow your head like you're deep in religious thought . . . but you're really flippin' to the right page. Ya read the answer, look up, an' give it to Karppi."

It was a daring plan. Cribbing answers right under the eyes of the minister and the whole Lutheran congregation had all the risks of dodging searchlights in a prison escape. But Carl was right. You couldn't see anyone's hands in the back row. It could be done if you had enough guts.

"There's one thing we better do," I said. "Practice."

"Practice what?" Carl asked.

"Practice flipping to the right page."

Early evening the following Monday, we were in Stumpy Bercanelli's Pool Hall in the basement below Anderson's Hardware Store where Carl worked, doing odd jobs like sweeping the floor, brushing the pool table felt, and emptying ash trays. Things were slow at the pool hall, so it was a good time to practice our catechism-page-flipping. It was Reino's turn to be tested.

"'When is swearing forbidden?'" Carl asked, looking up from his catechism.

Reino snapped to attention, his arms straight down, hands holding the catechism in front of his crotch. He squinted down at the book, furiously flipping pages. After several minutes, he looked up and said, "'Swearing is forbidden when it is done falsely, thoughtlessly, or in sinful, uncertain, or unimportant matters.'"

"Too slow," Carl said. "Ya gotta come up with the answer a lot faster'n that."

"There's over three hundred questions in this book," Reino complained. "I wuz lucky t'do it *that* fast."

"Can't you guys do yer lessons someplace else?" Stumpy squawked from behind the cash register, chomping on a smoldering cigar. The last thing in the world that Stumpy wanted was for the word to get out that he was harboring religious fanatics in his pool hall.

"We *gotta* work on this, Stumpy," Carl pleaded. "Look what we're up against." Carl took the catechism over to the counter and explained our strategy to Stumpy, hoping to rouse a little sympathy since Stumpy always enjoyed a good scam.

Puffing on his cigar, Stumpy thumbed through the book for several minutes. He puckered his bushy eyebrows in deep thought. Finally, he snapped his fingers. "Ya gotta be able t'get to the right page in a hurry, right? Here's what ya do . . . " He paused for dramatic effect, looking in turn at the three of us. "It's a li'l work, but not near as much as memorizin' all the answers . . . ya memorize the *page numbers* to the questions."

Eight weeks later, we were again gathered in the pool hall on a Saturday afternoon. Stumpy rolled his cigar over to the corner of his mouth with his tongue and cleared his throat as he looked up from the catechism lying open on the felt by a corner pocket on Table One. "What three creeds are used by the church?'" He shot a look at Carl and nodded curtly.

Without hesitation, Carl barked out his response like a marine recruit. "Page ninety-nine . . . " His fingers flew over the catechism down at arm's length. Finding the right page, he read quickly, looked up, and gave Stumpy the answer. "'The Apostles, the Nicene, and the Athanasian.'"

Stumpy checked his stopwatch. "Eight seconds . . . ain't too bad." He opened the book to another page and nodded at Reino. "For whom should we pray?'"

Reino bellowed out, "Page one-seventy-two . . . " His thumb scurried through the pages, pulling the catechism skillfully open at the proper place. "'We should pray for ourselves and for all other people, even for our enemies, but not for the souls of the dead.'"

"Seven seconds . . . tha's your best time so far," Stumpy said approvingly.

For the last two months we had worked tirelessly, memorizing page numbers for all the questions in the catechism, and we now responded like a team of well-trained commandos. We owed it all to Stumpy.

Stumpy had become thoroughly caught up in our catechism activity and had taken over the responsibility of coaching us. He had quickly deduced that the process really boiled down to eye-hand coordination, and he knew a lot about that. He often hosted a nickel-ante game of five-card-stud poker in the pool-hall storeroom for the benefit of the loggers. It was rumored that he was enjoying a phenomenal ten-year run of good cards.

Being Catholic, Stumpy didn't always agree with the precepts in the catechism, but that wasn't important. He'd drilled us over and over, through all the questions countless times until every page of our catechisms was frayed with use. He even introduced subtle improvements like putting tabs on every tenth page for quicker access.

Stumpy relit his cigar, blew a perfect smoke ring at the shaded light hanging over the pool table, and gave us a cool Knute Rockne stare. "Boys, tomorrah night's the big game. Remember everything I told ya . . . stay calm . . . keep yer head down . . . don't tip off yer play by squintin' or movin' yer shoulders when yer turnin' the pages. Ya done good over the past two months . . . I think you're ready. Maybe I'm prejudiced, but I think we're fieldin' the best catechism team that the Lutherans in this town will ever see."

Sunday night, the church basement was a hubbub of activity. Members of the volunteer group, the Luther Ladies, clucked around the confirmation candidates like mother hens, getting us ready for the ceremony.

The gowns in the traditional Bethany Lutheran colors of maroon with white trim were issued. I did a quick check on the billowing sleeves to verify that they were large enough to conceal the catechism when I held it. This didn't draw any attention, since everyone had their book out, getting in some last-minute cramming.

The strains of "Rock of Ages" filtered down from the balcony as Tulip Soumi warmed up on the pipe organ. Carl, Reino, and I, our hair glued fast with Wildroot Creme Oil and every pimple firmly cemented over with Clearasil, exchanged knowing glances and tight, nervous grins.

Pastor Karppi charged in and lined us up—girls first and the guys bringing up the rear. We marched up the stairs, following Karppi into the outer cloakroom, through the large double doors, and down the aisle.

Every pew was jammed to capacity, except for the two front ones reserved for us. I was surprised to see Stumpy Bercanelli sitting midway down on the aisle, looking strange in a suit and tie and without his cigar. Apparently, several other people also thought it was strange; necks were craning to look at him, as if he was some type of alien from a distant galaxy instead of a misplaced Catholic. It figured though—Stumpy had come to see his catechism team perform.

We took our seats, and Karppi strode up to the pulpit. He glanced up at the balcony and nodded, cuing Tulip Soumi at the organ. She blasted into a rousing rendition of "Onward Christian Soldiers," the standard opening number at our church functions. Tulip was especially partial to that song and literally pulled out all the stops. The stained-glass windows hummed with vibration, and even Pooter Kangas, who was as deaf as a post from standing too close to artillery pieces during World War I, began to tap his foot in time with the beat.

After the hymn, Karppi said a prayer and proceeded to give a stirring sermon on the everlasting merits of becoming a member of the Lutheran Church. He then motioned for the front pew occupants to come up and stand in front of the altar. As predicted by Carl, Karppi arranged us into two rows with the girls in front. Reino, Carl, and I were together in the middle of the back row—my grip was tight and sweaty on the catechism inside my right sleeve.

Karppi introduced each of us to the congregation and went directly into the questions, starting at one end of the front row.

I bowed my head reverently, furtively slipped the catechism out of the gown sleeve, and opened it at random. I looked down at the page and tried to focus my eyes—I couldn't see the print. The church lights were dim to begin with, and the cluster of bodies around me blocked off what little light there was. *It was too dark to read the book.*

Reino was standing directly on my right, and glancing over, I saw he also had his book open, down in the shadows. From the stricken look on his face I knew he had discovered the same problem. I could smell the fear percolating in our bodies. *We were doomed.*

Karppi was now quizzing the back row, firing off random shots on the Apostles' Creed. "Reino, what five points does the Third Article of the Creed discuss?"

Well, this is it. Reino would be the first one to have his monumental stupidity exposed. It's probably better this way—get the suffering over with.

Reino would be the first one to have his
monumental stupidity exposed.

"Page one-forty-four . . . ," Reino snapped, and then he stopped.

Nice try, Reino, but I think he's going to want more than the catechism page number.

Five seconds ticked off while Karppi, a sad, I-told-you-so smile playing on his lips, kept staring at Reino. I could almost hear Reino's brain grunting with exertion.

"'The Holy Spirit; the Church, the Communion of Saints; the Forgiveness of Sins; the Resurrection of the Body; and the Life Everlasting.'"

I gawked at Reino in disbelief. *How did he DO that? Had he actually been studying the answers on the sly and not telling me and Carl? It's pretty bad when you can't trust your best friend.*

Karppi's mouth was hanging open. He hadn't expected Reino to get the right answer either. Quickly gathering his composure, he directed his attention over to Carl. "Carl, why is it called the Apostles' Creed?"

"Page one-oh-one," Carl spit out in a loud voice. A pause, and then he continued. "'It is called the Apostles' Creed, not because it was written by the Apostles themselves but because it states briefly the doctrine which . . . the Creed is trinitarian because the Scriptures reveal . . . '"

I looked over at Carl while he was giving the answer, convinced he must be standing in a mysterious pool of light and able to *read* his catechism. But he wasn't even looking down at the book. He was staring straight ahead—trancelike—only his mouth moving.

I couldn't believe what I was seeing and hearing. Knowing Carl as they did, neither could some members of the congregation. A buzz rose from the crowd. Spud Kettu, Carl's uncle, who had spent the better part of the afternoon in the Spruce Grove Tavern, momentarily forgot where he was and broke into applause. Stumpy, thinking that this was customary in Lutheran churches, also started to clap his hands.

Pastor Karppi impatiently held up his hand for silence and fired off another question. "Gerald, how is human reason to be used in understanding Holy Scripture?"

He might as well have asked me how an atom bomb was made. I didn't have the foggiest idea what the answer was—all I remembered was the page number of the question. In panic, I looked out at the faces of the congregation. I locked eyes with Stumpy. Right then things got weird.

"Page fifty . . . ," my mouth was moving, but my brain wasn't concentrating on what I was saying. "'Holy Scripture is given in human language. To determine what it says we need to apply the rules of language, such as grammar and logic. It is right to use reason as a servant of the text, but the guidance of the Holy Spirit is essential for its proper understanding.'"

How did I do that? How could I say all that when I didn't know it? But it was my voice—what's going on? Was this what they call Divine Intervention? That's it! God is inside my head—Reino's and Carl's, too. He's going to make sure we get confirmed, and then He'll punish us for trying to cheat in church. He'll turn us over to the devil who'll give us an eternal assignment of memorizing an eight-zillion-page catechism.

Karppi was already back working on the front row, grilling the girls with a second round of questions. I was breathing in shallow gasps. What was going to happen when I got asked another question?

It didn't take long to find out. About five minutes later, Karppi asked me a second question. I found myself wanting to recite the page number again, but realizing that was sounding stupid, I held it back. I just stood there like a wooden Indian, not saying a word since I didn't know the answer.

Just as Karppi was ready to give up on me, I decided to blurt out the page number to show him that I had at least *looked* at the catechism. This must have triggered an automatic response from my memory because I spewed out the answer just as before.

It didn't take a genius to figure it out. Stumpy forced us over the stuff so many times that as we memorized the page numbers and practiced flipping through the catechism, we had accidentally memorized the answers. What had begun as another one of Carl Kettu's devious tricks had resulted in what we should have done in the first place.

And so it went. Karppi did three more rounds of questions, and Carl, Reino, and I, prefacing our responses with page numbers, came off like top-ranking divinity students. Finally, Pastor Karppi nodded at Tulip Soumi, who launched into "A Mighty Fortress Is Our God" on the organ. It was over. We were confirmed.

Coffee and refreshments were served in the church basement. The long table where we had slaved away so many Saturday mornings was decked out with a snowy-white tablecloth and loaded down with enough pastries to satisfy any Lutheran appetite. Stumpy made a quick exit after the ceremony since that was about as long as he could go without firing up a fresh cigar.

Carl, Reino, and I bathed in the glory of our success, getting our hands shook countless times. Most people were impressed that we knew the stuff so well that we could recite the page numbers, although Martha Paksu was overheard saying that she thought it was a cheap, smart-alecky stunt. That was probably just sour grapes.

Pastor Karppi was so taken with our performance that he came up to the three of us and asked if we might want to consider being mentors for the next confirmation class. Reino began to choke on a mouthful of jelly roll. I assured Karppi that we would give the offer a lot of thought.

Before I went to sleep that night, I said a little prayer of thanks—just something I thought up at the moment. If I had tried a fancy one like "The Lord's Prayer," I might have blurted out the page number, and I had pushed my luck far enough for one day.

The Great Cookie Conspiracy

M elvin Mulnik, the school woodshop teacher, balanced my pine board on meticulously manicured fingertips. He swung the board around to the window light, raising it to eye level as if inspecting a snifter of exquisite brandy. Sighting down the top surface, he carefully placed the blade of his carpenter's square at arm's length on the far end of the board and drew the square slowly toward himself, looking for any unevenness on the surface that I had just planed. I held my breath and snuck a peek over his shoulder.

Halfway down the board's length, he stopped; minuscule shafts of light had crept in under the square. His military mustache bristled with zeal.

"Aha . . . see that?" he cried. "You *still* have a high spot . . . right there." Whipping out a fancy mechanical drafting pencil, he marked an X on the board where the excess molecules of wood were located. "Plane this mark off, and it'll be just about right. I'll be back later to check it again." Mulnik marched over to the next workbench to demolish the ego of yet another suffering ninth-grade carpenter.

I stifled a curse and inserted the board back into the vise. Picking up my hand plane, I gingerly touched its blade, checking the setting and sharpness. Satisfied that the blade was now adjusted to peel off one-millionth of an inch of wood and sharp enough to shave the adolescent peach fuzz off my face, I carefully ran the plane over Mulnik's pencil mark. But the plane, by nature a perverse instrument, chomped into the board like a beaver biting a tree. Instead of a high spot, I now had a deep trough in the middle of the board.

Building a medicine cabinet was my woodworking project for this semester—not one of my smarter decisions. Including two shelves, the blueprint called for twelve boards. Mulnik demanded that the students plane all six surfaces of every board. Each surface then had to pass his personal inspection: pool-table flat—no lumps, bumps, dips, or chips. Sometimes it took seventeen planings and a week or more for him to approve one surface of one board. The more you plane a board, the smaller it gets, and if it gets too small, you have to chuck it and start over with a new board—I'd already planed three boards into oblivion. At this rate, I would be fifty by the time the medicine cabinet was finished.

Melvin Mulnik first appeared at our school at the beginning of November, replacing Clarence Hooker as the woodshop teacher after Hooker was promoted to high school principal. Mulnik had just retired from the army's Corps of Engineers where, according to his own admission, he had held a position of high responsibility. We'd never seen anyone quite like him. He had a stiff way of walking, like he had a two-by-four stuffed up the back of his shirt. He wore a suit and a sparkling-clean white shirt to school every day, and *he carried a briefcase.* Most people in our burg had never seen a briefcase before, and to them, it looked like a small suitcase. For the first two weeks, each time they saw him walking to school they thought he was leaving town.

Judging from the spit-and-polish way he took charge of the woodshop, Mulnik's army career must have been building desks for generals. He made it clear right from the outset that he wasn't going to let any half-assed woodcraft leave his shop. Every board had to be geometrically perfect; every flat-head-screw hole had to be precisely countersunk a prescribed depth known only to Mulnik and God; every varnished item had to have a mirror-like finish.

This was a jolting transition from woodshop under Clarence Hooker, who considered wood ready for construction use if the squirrels weren't living in it anymore and the sap had quit running out. Hooker's idea of a nice finish on a piece of woodcraft was a heavy coat of enamel to discourage the porcupines from chewing on it when you took your masterpiece out to deer camp. But those were bygone days, and we now suffered under the iron fist of Melvin Mulnik.

I took a break to settle my nerves and strolled over to Carl Kettu's bench. Carl was building a gun rack for his twenty-gauge shotgun. The rack was only one board with two pegs—a simple project that, under Mulnik's tutelage, he might even finish in a year or two. But on a scale of one to ten, Carl's woodworking skills ranked about minus four, and after thirty-eight planings, his board had shrunk like a bar of soap on a Saturday night.

"Gettin' pretty small, Carl," I observed. "Better start shopping around for a revolver."

Carl remained silent and tightened the vise across the edges of his board to replane the top side. The board was already dangerously thin, and as he turned the handle on the vise, the board buckled, snapped in two, and clattered to the floor.

Carl, riveted with shock, stared down at the corpse of his priceless gun rack like it was a lovable old pet dog that had suddenly died. "I been working on that board since before Thanksgiving," he sobbed.

"Tell Mulnik what happened," I said soothingly. "You kin start on another board, an' mebbe he'll go easy on the checking."

Carl wiped his eyes and looked wildly around the woodshop like a trapped animal. "Ain't gonna start over . . . gotta get outta this class . . . can't take it no more."

"You can't get outta woodshop," I said. "We gotta take it for two more years."

Our only vocational courses—woodshop and home economics—were mandatory from seventh through tenth grade at our little school squirreled away in the Upper Michigan woods. In the 1940's, the local educators considered it unlikely that any of us were going on to college, so the boys had to learn manual arts, and the girls, cooking and sewing.

"Who sez I gotta take it?" Carl yelled. "I'll . . . I'll take home ec. instead."

"Did you hear what you jus' said? Home ec.? That's fer *girls* . . . that's *cooking*."

Carl shuddered at the thought, but looking again at the two pieces of his gun rack on the floor, he made a decision. "So? Why can't *I* learn to cook?"

I edged away, putting some distance between us; the loss of his gun rack had jogged a couple of screws loose in Carl's brain—he could go berserk at any moment. "What's the matter with you?" I barked. "Snap out of it! Guys don't *cook*."

The next afternoon as I trudged wearily home from school, boots squeaking on the frozen December tundra, Carl ran up from behind and delivered a paralyzing punch to my upper arm, the standard greeting of teenage studs at the time. "I got in," he cried.

"Got in whut?"

"The home ec. class . . . I got in!"

"You got in the *home ec.* class?"

"Tha's right. No more planing up pine trees into shavings. I start tomorrow. I kin learn how t'cook easy, she sez."

"You talked Mrs. Bumford into lettin' *you* into the home ec. class? How'ja do that?"

Carl gave me a sly grin reserved for occasions when he had pulled off a brilliant coup. "'Member she jus' kicked her ol' man outta th'house . . . he wouldn't get a job . . . all he did wuz sit around all day and eat. She even hadda come home from school at noon an' cook fer him. I sez to her, 'I'd like t'learn t'cook. I think a guy ought'a be able t'take care of hisself instead'a always dependin' onna woman alla time t'feed him.' She gobbled that up . . . I knew she would. Later she told me that she went to see Schuyler about it. He didn't think much a the idea at first, I guess, but she kept sayin' that the school needed a more progressive education program, and he finally caved in."

"Whut's progressive education?"

"I dunno . . . who cares? All I know is, no more woodshop!"

A week later, Carl stopped me in the hallway between classes and handed me a cookie. "I jus' ran this off in home ec. class . . . try it."

I took a bite of the cookie. It was delicious. "You baked this?"

"Pretty good, huh?"

"*You* baked this? I repeated.

Carl shrugged. "Well . . . I hadda li'l help. Annette LaBeaute wuz workin' next t'me an' noticed that my cookie dough wuzn't lookin' quite like it oughtta, so she snuck me some of hers." Then Carl leaned over and added in a conspiratorial whisper, "An' tonight I'm gonna go over to her house fer sum advanced cookie lessons." He gave me a bright-eyed leer. "Who knows whut might happen while we're waitin' fer th'cookie dough to rise."

Annette LaBeaute, a ninth-grade, raven-haired knockout in possession of a twelfth-grade body, was in the thoughts and prayers of every guy in school. I swallowed a mouthful of saliva.

Carl saw that he had my undivided attention and gleefully pressed on. "This's great! All ya haft'a do is put a dumb look on your kisser, an' every girl in th'home ec. class wants t'help ya out." Y'know what I'm gonna be doin' Saturday night? Learnin' how t'thread a needle with Josephine Maki. I'm way behind on my sewin' an' may hafta spend a lotta time after school . . . heh, heh, heh."

He took a big bite out of a peanut butter cookie and smacked his lips loudly. "An' here's th'best part. I been passin' out cookies an' tellin' all the guys how great home ec. is, an' five or six a them wanna quit woodshop an' transfer over. Har, har, ol' Mulnik's gonna be wettin' his pants."

That wasn't exactly Melvin Mulnik's reaction to the situation when we gathered down in the woodshop the next day for our daily ritual of creating a knee-deep sea of wood shavings. Before we could get started, he herded us briskly through the doorway of his small office next to the shop.

"I've just come from a meeting in Superintendent Schuyler's office, and I understand that a number of you wish to follow in the misguided footsteps of young Mister Kettu and transfer over to home economics. I can only deduce that you find my woodworking standards a bit too rigorous and you feel that home economics will better suit your sluggish lifestyles." Mulnik's mustache twitched as he barked out each word, his granite eyes drilling into each one of us. "Well, you're going to get the opportunity to find out. Effective Monday, *all* of you will be transferred to Mrs. Bumford's home economics class for a period of two months."

A collective gasp.

Mulnik continued. "Of course, since Mrs. Bumford doesn't have the facilities up there to accommodate a huge class, and in the interest of fair play, it was decided that her girls will come down here and take up the basic principles of woodshop for that same period." His mouth twisted into a devious smile. "I sincerely hope that none of you fellows thought that the home economics class was going to be an opportunity to fraternize with the girls."

A collective whimper.

Monday morning, nine ex-carpenters perched on kitchen stools in the home economics room nervously waiting for Mrs. Bumford to make her entrance. Carl Kettu sat next to me nervously drumming his fingers on the spotlessly white table, babbling about how nice it was that we could join him.

But things were looking bad for Carl. With the exodus of the girls to woodshop, he was cut off from his newly found source of dates. Worse, he realized that he might actually have to *learn to cook*. Finally, some of the guys in our class wanted to take turns beating the snot out of him for getting us into this fix.

Everybody hated Mulnik, some thinking that he was probably an ex-Nazi and had really been in the German army—not ours. But woodworking was something that we had taken since the seventh grade, and it was second nature for most of us. Even the most boneheaded boy in school knew the basics of sawing, planing, and drilling wood. But cooking—that was up there with nuclear physics. Guys were not put on Earth to cook. After all, wasn't that why you got married?

Mrs. Bumford marched into the room and glared around at us like a drill sergeant. "Just a few words before we start. First of all, this wasn't my idea. Carl Kettu came to me a few weeks ago and wanted to join the class, and I thought there wasn't any harm in it. Why the rest of you decided it was a good idea still baffles me, but let me assure you, this class is no pushover. We'll be doing things that most of you have never done before. You'll clean up after yourselves. Even if you've never washed pots and pans before, you'll become experts at it in the next two months. Furthermore, we don't waste food, so at the end of each class, you eat what you cook . . . every last crumb."

Eat what you cook—a death sentence.

"Hey, Ham-Bone, try one a my cupcakes," I offered, plopping my latest culinary accomplishment into his mammoth paw.

Ham-Bone Huppala, a hulking monster of a kid with the proverbial strong back and weak mind, had become the group gourmand in the three weeks we had been slaving over hot stoves in home economics class.

He resided in a log cabin out on the Dead Dog River with his old man, a trapper. The two of them practically lived off the land, so Ham-Bone had been raised to eat anything even remotely organic. His sack lunches were gruesomely entertaining—sandwiches made from hardtack instead of bread, usually surrounding something unidentifiable, dark and oozing.

Consequently, anything we brewed up in home economics class, no matter how vile, was a taste treat to him. This was an extremely lucky break for us since everything had to be eaten before class was dismissed. Ham-Bone had always been a loner, but lately he had a lot of new friends since he would readily wolf down half-baked baking powder biscuits, petrified pancakes, or sixty-minute hard-boiled eggs.

Ham-Bone gave my cupcake his professional inspection. Cranking his mouth open, he tried to sink his huge yellow choppers into my masterpiece. They met with fierce resistance—the cupcake had the density of birch bark since I had forgotten to put in the shortening. Shifting his jaws into four-wheel drive, Ham-Bone really chomped down, biting the cupcake in two. He chewed noisily on it for a few seconds, looking thoughtfully up at the ceiling while he performed his taste test. "Y'put sum kinda nuts in it, didn'cha? I like nuts."

Actually, it was the eggshells that gave it that nutty consistency. For years I had watched my mother cracking eggs on the edge of bowls, never realizing what an art it was.

"Here, have some more," I urged. "I got three left."

Carl Kettu came dashing over to Ham-Bone's work table. "No . . . no . . . don't fill up on his cupcakes, Ham-Bone. Try one of mine." Carl had a large, flaky, black sphere in his hand—an eight ball with a skin disease. "I think I got the oven a li'l too hot."

While Ham-Bone was pondering the advisability of eating Carl's black cupcake, Mrs. Bumford came back into the room. It was common knowledge that she would occasionally slip away to the furnace room to have a cigarette, but ever since the boys had started taking home economics, she had been sneaking off with increasing regularity. This was probably to avoid excessive mental aggravation or possible lung damage due to the heavy pall of greasy smoke that hung in the room during our class time. She cast fatalistic glances at the array of mutant cupcakes on the work tables. Mrs. Bumford had long since given up tasting our food; visual inspections were enough—and a lot safer.

"Look," she wheezed, waving away the noxious burnt-cupcake fumes. "I'm going to try a different approach. Take your recipe books home . . . pick out something simple . . . get your mother, sister, aunt, or *anyone* to show you how to cook it. When you come to class on Wednesday, you'll try it yourself. Now, finish eating your food and get started washing the dishes."

Ham-Bone flipped Carl's cupcake onto his work table. It bounced a couple of times, rolled drunkenly to the edge, and fell off, hitting the floor with a clank. "I ain' gonna eat thet thing unless ya gimme a nickel first," he said to Carl.

If Mrs. Bumford thought she had problems, they were small potatoes compared to what had been going on in woodshop. Melvin Mulnik was convinced there was absolutely no reason why girls couldn't turn out the same quality of woodcraft as boys. Given enough time he was probably right, but he had inherited a group of girls that included some who had never so much as held a hammer. He put them to work right away building bookcases and the like, not realizing that most of them couldn't drive a nail into a board without mashing the finger that held it. Girls who thought a plane was something you went to the Marquette Airport to see were expected to make a board so smooth it would pass Mulnik's window-light test. Needless to say, there was a lot of complaining, much screeching, and more than a little blood spilled.

There was one basic difference between boys and girls taking woodshop. A boy would never think of going home and complaining about Mulnik because it was very likely his old man had built the house they lived in and he could expect no sympathy. However, when the girls brought home horror stories about woodshop and displayed mangled fingers, the reaction was quite different.

Peculiar things began to happen to Mulnik. One morning after a particularly heavy snowfall, Mulnik couldn't find his Model A coupe. He knew he had left it at the side of the road in front of his house, but now it was nowhere to be seen. Finally, around two in the afternoon, after the sun had melted some of the snow, the roof of his car appeared out of an unusually large snowbank in front of his house. It seemed that Arne Millimaki, our township snowplow operator, whose daughter Alice was currently taking woodshop from Mulnik, had inadvertently covered up the Model A when he plowed the road that morning. This was very odd because Arne was considered a real

After the sun had melted some of the snow, the roof of his car appeared out of an unusually large snowbank.

99

artist with the snowplow. He could thread a needle with a load of snow and always took great pains not to push snow on people's cars. It was doubly unfortunate since the passenger-side window had been accidentally left open, and the inside of the Model A was packed tight with snow.

A few days later some town wag had decided that Mulnik's woodpile should set an example for fine woodwork. During the night, Mulnik's two cords of firewood—prime maple logs—had been spirited away from the side of his house. Each log, beautifully planed flat on four sides, was carefully stacked back in Mulnik's yard before sunrise. Everyone agreed it was the best-looking stack of firewood in town. However, the planing reduced the wood to less than a cord, so there was some speculation as to whether Mulnik would have enough left to last through the cold snap we always got in April. Some suspicion fell on Toivo Neimi, who did cabinet work around town. Toivo, whose daughter Elma was also in Mulnik's woodshop class, owned a power planer, and it would take something like that to plane up two cords of wood overnight.

Mulnik got pretty upset and went to see Superintendent Schuyler, claiming there was a town conspiracy against him. Schuyler scoffed at the idea and told Mulnik that people just got a little frisky waiting for the long winter to end and that everything would calm down once the weather warmed up.

Wednesday morning arrived. This was the day that everyone brought in their *homework* recipes that we were to cook by ourselves. The atmosphere in the classroom was fairly bristling with essences of scorched spaghetti, overly scrambled eggs, and hash flambé.

The fragrance issuing from Ham-Bone's pot—a biting gaminess with a hint of burnt fur—was particular interesting.

Mrs. Bumford tentatively approached the stove where Ham-Bone was industriously stirring his large, simmering pot. "What are you cooking, Walter?" she asked, using Ham-Bone's given name.

Ham-Bone continued to agitate the pot's ingredients with a large wooden spoon. "This's my ol' man's favorite," he stated proudly. "Calls it *Bush Stew.*"

"I see . . . ah . . . what's in it?"

"Spuds, sum carrots, dandelion greens, a pinch of coffee grounds, chopped up pine cones . . . my ol' man sez pine cones keeps ya regular . . . an' meat."

Mrs. Bumford thought long and hard before she asked the next question. "What kind of meat?"

Ham-Bone carefully ladled up a steaming spoonful of oily, brown sludge. "Why don'cha taste it first?"

Mrs. Bumford twitched reflexively. "Ah . . . well . . . yes . . . maybe later." She hurried over to the next stove where Carl Kettu was adjusting the oven temperature controls. "What's that you're baking, Carl?"

"Peanut butter cookies, Miz Bumford. I think they're jus' about done. Wanna try one?"

"Why don't I take a look at them first?"

Carl grabbed a hot pad, opened up the oven door, snatched one of the dozen cookies on the tray, and put it on a plate.

Mrs. Bumford carefully looked the cookie over. She picked it up and put it near her nose, a habit she had recently acquired. "It smells very good, Carl." She took a tentative bite, chewed a moment, and smiled. "Why, that's delicious, Carl. However did you do so well?"

"Workin' close with my mom, Miz Bumford," Carl said studiously. "I think anybody kin cook good if they're willin' to work hard at it."

Mrs. Bumford polished off the rest of the cookie. "Amazing. The rest of you boys should take a lesson from Carl . . . he's really learning how to cook." She moved on to the next stove where fried oatmeal was being featured.

Grinning with relief, Carl reopened the oven door and pulled out his tray of cookies. Mutt Hukala reached over, grabbed one of Carl's cookies, and popped it in his mouth. He immediately spit it out. "Gahhk! What'za matter with Bumford? This thing tastes like a horse turd."

Carl quickly put the tray of cookies down on the table and tried to silence Mutt. "Keep it down. I didn't give her one *I* made . . . I slipped her one of *these*." He selected another cookie from the tray and gave it to Mutt.

Mutt took a small bite, looked at Carl, and gobbled up the rest of the cookie. "Okay, where'dja get this cookie?"

"My ma baked 'em las' night . . . I smuggled a few a them in here. Sneaked 'em onto my cookie sheet an' put 'em in the oven a coupl'a minutes before Bumford came around t'check my stuff."

Mutt reached over to grab another cookie but then stopped. He stared hard at the tray, trying to figure out which cookies were baked by Carl's mother.

Elated over Carl's success with the peanut butter cookies, Mrs. Bumford knew that she was on the right track letting the boys research cooking projects at home. She made a similar assignment for the following Monday.

Never one to let well enough alone, Carl became even more brazen. On Monday, he made up the dough for a batch of molasses cookies in class, but at the last minute furtively dumped it in the garbage can, arranged two dozen of his mother's molasses cookies on the baking tray, and slipped the tray into the oven. Timing it just right to match Mrs. Bumford's rounds, Carl heated up the oven so the cookies were deliciously warm for her inspection. She loved them. Seizing the opportunity to justify her decision to let him transfer into home economics, Mrs. Bumford took great delight in spreading the word among the faculty that Carl Kettu was the school's undisputed cookie king.

In the weeks to follow, Carl scored other victories, sticking mostly with cookies or an occasional muffin because they were the easiest to smuggle into class and reheat. Of course, the other eight guys in the class didn't enjoy Carl's status. We knew all about his switching scam, but since our First Commandment at school was "Thou shalt not squeal," his secret was safe.

We finally got to the end of the two-month sentence of home economics, and it seemed that the experiment was a limited success. Most of us had progressed to the point where we could *almost* eat our own cooking without gagging. Mrs. Bumford, on days when she was feeling brave, would even sample our wares.

Mrs. Bumford strode into our last class. "Well, you're going to get a chance to show off. Mr. Schuyler has requested that our class prepare the refreshments for the monthly faculty meeting. He asked that it be done completely by the boys in this class . . . I can't participate."

She paused, waiting for reactions, and smiled when she saw the fear in our eyes. "I know what you're thinking . . . you'll mess this up. Don't worry . . . fortunately Carl can pull us through this just fine. If he can whip up a couple of batches of his wonderful cookies and someone can brew some halfway decent coffee, you'll do just fine. How about it, Carl?"

"Of course, Miz Bumford," Carl purred confidently. "I kin knock together two or three batches of cookies . . . no problem. What day is this faculty meeting gonna be?"

"Today . . . at four o'clock . . . two hours from now. It's going to be at Miss Parsons' house, so we'll have to get started right away. We'll take whatever you need over there in my car. Since we don't need the entire class, Carl will pick two helpers and the rest of the class will go to study hall."

"Two hours?" Carl squeaked.

"*Whatarewegonnado?*" Carl hissed. "I can't make cookies." Carl had chosen me and Ham-Bone to be his helpers, and we were in the home economics pantry loading up a box with cookie-making material to take to Miss Parsons' house.

"Well, I guess you're gonna have to whomp up somethin' anyhow, unless you kin figure out a way to sneak your ma into Parsons' kitchen."

"I'll make th'coffee," Ham-Bone boomed cheerfully. "My ol' man showed me how t'make real good coffee."

Carl grabbed my arm. "You're a smart guy . . . you kin probably make good cookies, huh?"

"You kiddin? I've made oatmeal, scrambled eggs, boiled potatoes, baked beans, hamburgers, cupcakes, and tapioca pudding in this class, and when I taste 'em I can't tell the difference."

Carl got a grip on his composure. "Jeez, what am I worried about? It's only a few cookies fer crissake. What could go wrong?"

Annabelle Parsons, our high school English teacher, lived in a large Victorian house on the edge of the Michigamme River with her sister, Martha. No kid had ever seen the inside of the house since Miss Parsons wasn't disposed to socialize with adolescent riff-raff after she had slaved all day trying to beat the principles of diagramming sentences into their thick skulls. Once a month she would host the faculty business meeting in her parlor. Usually the refreshments consisted of peanut cakes, rhubarb pie, and jelly rolls, all baked by Martha.

But Mrs. Bumford had made such a big ballyhoo about Carl's cookies that this time Mr. Schuyler had stuck her with the job. This was a lofty honor since Mr. Schuyler thought very highly of Martha Parson's baked wares.

We pulled up in Mrs. Bumford's car and unloaded the supplies. Mrs. Bumford was in a highly charged state, anticipating a triumphant afternoon taking compliments for Carl's culinary delights. "The kitchen door is open, so you can get started right away," she chirped as we went up the sidewalk. "Miss Parsons is still at school, and her sister went out visiting, so there's no one around to distract you."

We carried the cookie makings into the kitchen. There, in front of us, was the biggest damned wood stove I had ever seen in my life. It had about fifty lids on it and an oven large enough to easily bake a plow horse. It was also stone cold.

"You better get that stove going," Mrs. Bumford said. "Those cookies will have to be served in an hour and a half."

"It's a wood stove," Carl blurted. The stoves in class were gas with oven temperature controls.

Mrs. Bumford looked at him sharply. "Isn't this like the stove you and your mother have been working with at home?"

"Oh . . . yeah . . . yeah . . . I jus' never seen one so big . . . that's all. Don' worry 'bout a thing, Miz Bumford, we'll have those cookies out in no time."

"Well then, I've got to get back to the school. All the faculty will be over here in an hour. We'll be meeting out in the parlor so nobody will be bothering you until we take the break for refreshments." Mrs. Bumford opened the kitchen door. "I'll see you later. Good luck."

After she left, the three of us stood there for a minute, looking at the humongous inert mass of cold cast iron from which mouth-watering cookies were to be forthcoming in ninety minutes. "I think you should have confessed," I said to Carl.

"Maybe we should hitchhike outta town," said Ham-Bone. "We could be at the Wisconsin border by the time they get here."

Ham-Bone and I lugged in firewood while Carl scratched his head over the recipes. Mrs. Bumford had suggested that he bake one batch of his famed peanut butter cookies and a batch of molasses cookies.

Carl glanced up from the recipes. "The molasses cookie recipe sez set th'oven for 350 degrees, and the peanut butter cookies need 375 degrees. This thing ain't gotta temperature doohickey on it. What'll we do?"

What does yer ma do?" I asked.

"I dunno . . . I think she jus' throws in a lotta wood till the oven gets hot."

"That's what we'll do, then."

Ham-Bone was a great hand at building fires and in no time at all had a good one going in the wood stove. But the oven took its own sweet time getting hot, and time was running out.

Following the recipe, Carl put some molasses in a big pan and put it on the stove top to boil. "It'll go a lot faster if you put it over the open fire," Ham-Bone suggested.

Carl took off one of the stove lids, and flames shot into the air. He set the pan over the open hole. The hot fire licked greedily around the pan, blackening it while attempting to get at the molasses.

Meanwhile I decided to make my contribution by mixing the ingredients for the peanut butter cookies in a big bowl. I threw in an extra cup of peanut butter to make sure the cookies had that good peanut-buttery flavor. The combination of lard, butter, peanut butter, two different kinds of sugars, and one egg quickly congealed into an impenetrable lump with the consistency of hardening concrete.

"It sez t'sift in the flour . . . whazzat mean?" I cried out.

Prob'ly a mistake in spelling," Carl shot back. "I think it means *lift*. Jus' dump 'er in."

Ham-Bone was chucking wood into the stove like Casey Jones stoking up his locomotive. The stove pipe was taking on a dull red glow, looking like a giant hot rivet. The temperature in the kitchen was inching upward, and we stripped off our shirts as the action picked up.

I dumped flour, baking powder, baking soda, and salt onto the mass of peanut butter cookie dough, giving it the appearance of a cow plop in a snow storm. I tried to mix it up with a spoon, but the spoon would only sink in an inch or so before the dough held it fast. "I can't get the white stuff mixed into the dough."

Carl scowled at the dough and scratched himself. "I saw a hammer out in the storm porch. Pound it in."

The hammer produced much better results than the spoon—I whacked the cookie dough into submission.

"Now it sez *chill*." I yelled. "Do I put it in the refrigerator?"

"It'll chill a helluva lot faster outside," Ham Bone volunteered. "It's 'bout ten below zero out there."

That made sense, so I put the bowl of dough out on the back steps.

The molasses on the stove was in a raging boil, hissing and snapping like a treed raccoon. Carl grabbed the handle of the pan to take it off the fire, but forgot to use a hot pad. He let out a scream of pain, and the pan of molasses hit the floor, spilling out half the contents. Ham-Bone displayed excellent presence of mind, grabbing a spoon and scraping much of the molasses back into the pan before it had a chance to seep into the wood.

"Better add in a li'l more to be on the safe side," I said.

"Good idea," Ham-Bone replied, and he glugged in another half pint of molasses into the pan.

The stove was now roaring along at full throttle, flames leaping up through the seams in the cast-iron top. The kitchen was as hot as an iron smelter, so we unbuttoned and peeled down the tops of our long underwear, leaving them hanging down over our pants. Carl mixed the rest of the ingredients into the molasses while I greased the cookie sheets with butter. Everything was going fine except for one minor incident. Ham-Bone accidentally stepped in the hardening puddle of molasses on the floor, and his foot pulled out of his shoe. Deciding that it wasn't a good idea to track molasses around the floor, he left the shoe there.

"Omigawd!" I remembered the peanut butter cookie dough out on the back steps. I ran out and picked up the icy-cold bowl. The dough sparkled with frost and was as hard as granite. I tapped it a couple of good ones with the hammer, and the bowl split in half. "I'm supposed to roll this stuff into balls, an' it's as solid as a rock." I moaned.

"There's an axe out at the woodpile," offered Ham-Bone.

I got the axe and put the frozen cookie dough on the kitchen table. Grabbing the axe halfway up the handle, I gave the dough a couple of tentative chops, but the axe blade only creased it. Deciding that I needed more force, I raised the axe over my head and gave the dough a good whack. This was too much for the kitchen table—the table legs collapsed, and the cookie dough skittering along the floor like a large, peanut-butter-colored hockey puck. There was no time to fix the table. I put on my jacket and took the cookie dough out to the chopping block next to the woodpile. It did the trick, and I hacked the dough into small hunks, although none of them looked much like balls. I gathered them up in an empty potato sack and was bringing them into the kitchen just as Carl was putting out the molasses cookie dough to chill.

"Forget the chilling," I said. "It's too much trouble."

Carl's molasses cookie dough looked like oil-pan drainings I had seen over at Chub Mattila's Standard Station. At least it was more manageable than my peanut butter dough. He started to roll it out with the rolling pin. It was a bit on the sticky side, probably due to the extra shot of molasses that Ham-Bone had added, and for a minute we didn't think that Carl was going to get the rolling pin loose from the dough. Finally, he got the cookies carved out with a Mason-jar lid.

Meanwhile, Ham-Bone started on the coffee. He found Mrs. Parsons' monstrous coffeepot, filled it up with water, and dumped in two pounds of coffee.

"Don'cha think that's an awful lot of coffee t'be usin'?" I asked.

"My ol' man alwuz sez thet coffee ain't worth a damn unless it grows hair on yer eyeballs," Ham-Bone replied cheerfully, as he broke four eggs on the rim of the open pot and chucked them in, shells and all.

"*Eggs* in th'coffee?" Carl and I asked, in unison.

Ham-Bone took off one of the stove lids and placed the pot over the open fire. "A course! Don't everybody? Eggs gives th'coffee sum body, my ol' man sez. It's th'only way we drink it."

Carl laid out his molasses cookies on one of the cookie sheets, and I put the peanut butter cookies on the other. "Let's check out the oven," I said as I leaned down and opened the oven door. A scorching blast of heat seared my eyeballs.

"Ya think it's 350 degrees yet?" Carl asked.

"I'd say it's just about right," I replied, blinking my eyes to get them back in focus. We slid the cookie sheets in and closed the oven door.

"The recipes say that the molasses cookies should bake for five to seven minutes, but the peanut butter cookies need ten to twelve minutes," Carl said. "What'll we do?"

"I say we ought'a leave 'em both in for fifteen minutes, just to be on the safe side," I said. "No sense havin' half-baked cookies."

The coffee was boiling over through the spout. Ham-Bone grabbed the pot with a hot pad and put it on the counter. He poured himself a cup and took a sip. "Ah . . . now thet's gooooood coffee," he said with a sigh.

It had been a long afternoon. I needed a jolt of caffeine, so I poured myself a cup, not paying much attention to the looks of the coffee coming out of the pot. I took a deep swallow.

The coffee paused only briefly in my stomach, rushing directly into the blood stream. My heart stopped momentarily and then began to race out of control. I tried to speak, but the neural connectors between my brain and vocal cords had melted down. Finally, I rasped to Ham-Bone, "Y-y-you   c-c-can't s-s-serve t-t-this."

The door from the parlor opened, and Mrs. Bumford charged into the kitchen. "It's time to serve the refresh . . . " She spotted the flames shooting up through the cracks in the stove top. "Quick . . . get a pail of water . . . put out that fire!" she yelled, pointing at the stove.

"No . . . no," Carl interjected. Everything's all right. The cookies are bakin' in the oven right now."

Mrs. Bumford's beautifully waved hair started to unwind from the stove heat, and her pancake makeup began sliding off her face. Open-mouthed, she gawked at the kitchen table lying in a heap on the floor—Ham-Bone's shoe resting in the puddle of molasses—dirty and broken dishes strewn around—the three of us bare-chested, all smeared with flour and molasses. "Wha . . . wha . . . "

Carl flashed her a reassuring smile as he struggled back into his long underwear top. "Well, you know what they say, Miz Bumford. You can't be a good cook without dirtying a few dishes." Speaking in soothing tones, he gently spun her around, and ushered her back out through the parlor door.

Smoke was billowing out of the oven, so we opened the oven door and yanked the cookie sheets out. You would not have mistaken these cookies for the ones Carl's mother had made.

The peanut butter cookies that I had painstakingly shaped with the axe now bore an uncanny resemblance to the rusting chunks of iron ore you could find next to the railroad tracks—dark, flinty edges—razor sharp to the touch.

The molasses cookies were more striking in appearance—even aesthetically pleasing. They had been fired into a black shiny finish, and the light from the stove fire cast weird reflections off them. They looked like giant, three-inch tiddlywinks.

All the cookies were stuck fast to the cookie sheets, but we found a large screwdriver in the storm porch and chiselled them loose. It was obvious they had been somewhat overbaked and were perhaps a little on the tough side, but this was no time to dwell on details.

Carl and I loaded the cookies on plates while Ham-Bone got the coffee cups and saucers from the cupboard. We quickly put our shirts back on, carefully combed our hair, and lugged the faculty refreshments into the parlor.

There were eight or nine teachers there having a spirited debate over what size shot Emil, the school custodian, should use in his shotgun shells for blasting down the six-foot icicles clinging to the school eaves—a chronic Upper Michigan late-winter problem. Last year he used buckshot and blew off large chunks of the roof.

We set the cookies, coffeepot, cups, and saucers down on Miss Parsons' library table. Ham-Bone began to pour coffee. Mrs. Bumford, already badly shaken, took one look at the cookies, scrabbled around in her purse, and fished out a cigarette—odd, since she never smoked in public.

Miss Parsons stared in disbelief at the coffee strainer that Ham-Bone held over each cup as he poured. Huge lumps of coffee grounds imbedded with eggshells tumbled into it. The strainer wasn't enough, however, to catch the egg yolk material that floated to the top of each cup, creating a toxic-looking, yellow oil slick.

Ichabod Schuyler, the school superintendent, jutted out prominently in the group with his six-foot-four-inch bony frame—all kneecaps, elbows, and extraordinarily long fingers. With two of these fingers he plucked a molasses cookie off the plate and turned it over carefully. He studied it with a quizzical, scientific interest. He rapped it lightly on the edge of the library table—rapped it harder—took it in the fingers of both hands and tried to bend it. A troubled scowl drifted across Schuyler's craggy face as it dawned on him that he was to be denied his one monthly gratification, the faculty meeting refreshments. He spoke to Carl. "Did you make this?"

Carl nodded silently.

Schuyler continued. "Carl, you were the first one to transfer from woodshop to the home economics class, were you not?"

Carl nodded again.

Schuyler thought for a second. Then, as if he had found a way to amuse himself in an otherwise disappointing situation, his expression brightened. He turned to Mrs. Bumford. "Mrs. Bumford . . . since you are responsible for these . . . these *cookies* being here, you should have the honor of the first taste." Schuyler picked up the plate of molasses cookies and shoved it in front of Mrs. Bumford.

Mrs. Bumford stared at the pile of cookies like it was a nest of rat-tlesnakes. She shook her head violently. "Uh . . . no . . . no, thank you."

Schuyler swung the plate around to Mulnik. "How about you, Mr. Mulnik? You've also had an indirect hand in this affair."

"Of course," Mulnik said crisply, as he reached for a molasses cookie. His military training had prepared him for dangerous assignments. He bit the cookie—then bit harder—finally biting down as hard as he could, the cords in his neck bulging out with the exertion. With an audible crack, the cookie relinquished a piece of itself to Mulnik's mouth.

Mulnik crunched the cookie with extreme concentration. All eyes in the room were fixed on his jaws. With an arduous effort, he swallowed. It was only then that the flavor of the cookie registered with his taste buds. He tried to breathe but could only gasp and choke.

Schuyler now smiled wickedly. "Perhaps one of the other cookies would be more to your liking." He grabbed one of the peanut butter cookies, wincing as a sharp cookie edge punctured his fingertip. Mulnik, red-faced, could only shake his head vigorously. "Then, maybe you you'd like some coffee to wash that down," Schuyler said. "There's nothing worse than eating cookies dry."

Mulnik thought coffee was an excellent idea. He snatched a cup of Ham-Bone's coffee off the library table and took a great big gulp.

It was good to be back in woodshop. I whistled joyously as I faced the window light and checked the evenness of the medicine chest's top board with the carpenter's square. Satisfied that it was ready for inspection, I took it over to Clarence Hooker who was filling in as woodshop teacher until they could find a replacement for Mulnik.

Mulnik's heart and nerves had gotten nearly back to normal after an hour or so on Miss Parsons' parlor couch, but the Monday following the faculty meeting, he turned in his resignation to Schuyler. By then he was totally convinced the cookies were part of the town's conspiracy against him. He claimed that he was going to reenlist in the army where he would be treated with some respect.

"Would you like to check this board, Mr. Hooker? I just got through planing it."

Hooker ran his thumb over the board to see if he picked up any splinters, nodded his head, and handed it back to me.

I reached back and flung the molasses cookie far out over the cedar swamp at the edge of town. It skimmed nicely over the trees. Carl jerked the twenty-gauge shotgun to his shoulder and fired. The cookie shattered in midair.

"Nice shot," I said, as I reached in the bag for another cookie. Carl had retrieved the cookies from the faculty meeting, figuring there might be some use for them. He was right. Clay pigeons were expensive, and the molasses cookies made excellent substitutes. The peanut butter cookies didn't have as good aerodynamic qualities, but Carl claimed that when he put them out in his woodshed, the rats nibbled on them and moved out. I think he was making that up, though.

I threw another molasses cookie over the cedar trees. Carl fired. The cookie jerked but continued on its flight.

"Did'ja hit it? I think you missed," I said.

"Naw . . . I hit it," Carl said dryly, as he pumped another shell into the chamber. "Some of them cookies're jus' tougher than others."

Lust in the Slush

Winter had brought with it the *Christmas card* snow, sparkling-white and crunchy to the touch. It squeaked musically beneath your feet—a beautiful cover over an otherwise barren landscape. But now it was late March—the slush season—a dreary time of year in Upper Michigan. The first weeks of spring still saw snow on the ground, but it had aged ungracefully, taking on a diseased color and texture—flecked with ice crystals—black and brown around the edges from chimney soot and passing cars. The longer days had turned the snow into slush, blending with the mud on the roads to form the frosty, ugly soup of springtime.

There wasn't much to do during slush season. Kids were bored—too late for skiing, trapping, and basketball—too early for marbles and baseball. Housewives waited anxiously for the ground to dry so they could drag the rugs out to the backyard clothesline for their annual spring beating. Men took a depressive inventory of the havoc wreaked by the winter's road salt on the fenders and rocker panels of the family Ford or Chevy, vowing to invest in undercoating on the next new car.

This March, 1949, I approached my sixteenth birthday. The mysterious forces of puberty were at work within my body, about to disrupt the normal chain of events during this slush season.

A few of us were hanging around the lube rack in Chub Mattila's Standard Station watching Chub change the oil in a rare '42 DeSoto. Reino Rovaneimi was inspecting the station's new punchboard in the hopes of hitting the fifty-dollar jackpot so he could quit the tenth grade and retire.

"Yer still cherry, ain'tcha?" Mutt Hukala asked me.

Without thinking, I held up my bottle of soda pop. "Nope . . . it's strawberry."

Reino looked up from the punchboard and guffawed loudly.

I realized my error. "Oh . . . heh, heh . . . well, you know . . . I'm still lookin' over th'girls in town . . . "

Mutt, with his characteristic street-smart bluntness, was referring to the fact that at the ripe old age of sixteen, I was, to put it politely, *uninitiated.* In 1949, this was no big deal, but it was nevertheless a delicate topic. Except for an on-going crush on the stunning Mildred Spagarelli, a freshman at Republic High School, I had so far frittered away early adolescence on model airplane building, weasel trapping, and trying to learn how to dribble a basketball. To be sure, I had noticed that the sweaters of my female classmates were starting to pooch out and the meaner ones who used to beat the pee out of me were losing some of their upper-arm muscle tone. But so far, these phenomena didn't merit in-depth consideration.

"Yeah, I thought so," Mutt said. "You need help. On yer own, ya won't get any till yer forty years old."

"Help?"

Mutt lit up a Lucky. "Yeah, I'm goin' down to Bertha's Monday night. Y'wanna come along?"

"Who's Bertha?"

Mutt snorted the smoke out of his nostrils. "Gawdamn. You gotta quit spendin' so much time on that trap line an' start rubbin' elbows with people instead a weasels. You ain't heard a Bertha's down in Hoot Owl?"

Hoot Owl was a small, wide-open Wisconsin town just across the state line. For years I had lurked on the fringes of groups of older guys talking about it at the station. The legal drinking age in Wisconsin was eighteen, but in Hoot Owl you only had to be tall enough to reach the top of the bar with your money. And the women—guys rolled their eyes when they discussed them in reverent tones. Did you want one that looked like Hedy Lamarr? Mae West? Whatever your taste, they had it in Hoot Owl.

Mutt kept looking at me, a wicked smile creeping onto his face. "Well? Y'wanna come along or not?"

Nobody had ever invited *me* to go to Hoot Owl. My imagination did a few erotic cartwheels, but the part of my brain in charge of fear of the unknown was putting the brakes on. "Uh . . . I dunno . . . "

Reino cackled and chimed in with one of his usual diplomatically phrased observations. "He's chicken, Mutt."

Even Chub came out from underneath the DeSoto on the rack, wiping his hands, grinning, and waiting for my answer.

Mutt leaned in and, in a hoarse whisper dripping with lust, said, "The las' time I wuz in Bertha's, there wuz a girl there that looked jus' like Mildred Spagarelli, 'cept better built."

That did it—I nodded. "Okay."

Mutt whipped his head around. "How 'bout you, Rovaniemi? We kin always use 'nother to chip in fer gas."

Reino just stood there, his pimples glowing in the stark florescent light, his mouth partially open. "Uh . . . maybe next time."

"Th'women at Bertha's kin *cure* those pimples."

"What time on Monday?" Reino asked.

Mutt had outstanding powers of persuasion.

"Reino, kin I ask ya a question?" The two of us were walking home from the Standard Station.

"What?"

"Uh . . . well . . . d'ya know what to do when yer with th'women at a place like Bertha's?"

"What to do? Whaddaya . . . stoopid?"

"No, no, I don' mean that . . . I mean . . . do ya shake hands an' introduce yerself . . . or jus' pay 'em an' take yer clothes off . . . pay 'em later . . . make conversation . . . tell 'em jokes, or what?"

Reino absently fingered a prize-winning pimple on his jaw. "How should I know? I ain't been there either . . . I do know one thing, though . . . we better bring rubbers."

"Oh, yeah. That's right. Ya got any?"

"Nope. I imagine Otto sells 'em at his drugstore."

"Otto? We can't buy 'em from Otto . . . th'whole town'll know about it. We'll haf'ta go down the road to DePaul's in Ishpeming to get 'em."

Reino winced in pain as he squeezed the pimple. "Guess so . . . jus' remember they don't call 'em rubbers in the drugstore."

"Whadda they call 'em?"

"Boy, ya don't know nuthin' 'bout sex, do ya? They call 'em *prolifics*."

I fished some paper out of my shirt pocket. "Lemme write that down."

Saturday morning, Reino and I pulled up to DePaul's Drugstore in old man Rovaniemi's car. We stood on the sidewalk for a minute plotting our strategy.

"*You* buy 'em," Reino said. "Ain't no sense both of us botherin' the clerk. Besides, ya owe me for some gas anyhow."

"Boy, an' you called *me* a chicken." We looked up and down the street and skulked into the drugstore.

The only clerk in DePaul's was a woman. I executed a sharp one-eighty turn and went back out the door, Reino close behind.

"Whatzamatter?" Reino asked.

"You crazy? I ain't gonna buy 'em from a *woman*. Erickson's Drugs is over on Main. Let's try there."

Fortunately, there was a guy in a white pharmacist's jacket behind the counter in Erickson's. I sidled up to the counter. "I'd like some prolifics," I said quickly, in a low voice.

The pharmacist gave me a strange look. "What?"

A little gray-haired lady came up and stood behind me with a pre-scription sheet in her hand.

I ratcheted my voice down another notch. "I'd like some prolifics."

A glint of recognition. "Prophylactics? *That's* what you want?" his voice vibrated the front windows. The little old lady's eyes burned holes in my back.

"Yeah, that's it. Medium size."

"They only come in one size . . . fits everybody," he boomed. "What brand do you want?"

A severe tic was developing under my right eye. "Uh . . . anything. Don' make any difference."

He reached under the counter and brought out two packets. "This is the most popular brand," he screamed. "They give you a choice. Lubricated or unlubricated . . . which'll it be?"

I looked down at the packets sitting naked on the counter. They were growing in size by the second, threatening to engulf the store at any moment. I pointed at one of them.

"How many would you like?" he yelled.

My brain seized up. *How many would I like?* I didn't have a clue.

"You get a good price on a dozen," he volunteered.

"Yeah . . . okay . . . a dozen." Then I remembered Reino. "Make that two dozen."

I gathered up Reino at the magazine rack, looking at comic books. "Forget the comic books. What you need is a dictionary. *Prolifics* . . . jeezus."

Since Reino and I both realized that we were total imbeciles about sex, I figured that a little education was in order. So while Reino was driving us home on US-41, I tore open the foil on one of the packets and pulled out the prophylactic. It was rolled up tightly. It made sense that if you were going to get them ready for use, they had to be unrolled. So I unrolled—and unrolled some more. When it was ten inches long, Reino glanced over at it. He had an instant anxiety attack, losing control of the car and almost taking out three roadside mailboxes in West Ishpeming. Surely the pharmacist must have been wrong. They had to come in different sizes.

At six-thirty Monday night, the three of us were heading south on Highway M-95 in Mutt's '32 Plymouth, trailing a huge blue exhaust plume like a crippled Japanese Zero. Perched in the back seat, I was getting a vigorous massage from the unbalanced rear tires. Next to me was a large cardboard box containing all the essentials for the fifty-mile journey—an inner-tube patching kit, a tire pump, a five-gallon can of water to use when the radiator reached its usual boil, and three quarts of used oil that Chub had donated. It would have been foolish to buy new oil since it didn't stay in the engine long enough to get acquainted with the pistons.

My stomach was losing its battle with a rapidly congealing mass of meat loaf and mashed potatoes—I made a mental note never to eat a heavy supper the next time my virginity was on the line. Fortunately, I was getting a lot of fresh air since we were running with all windows down to suck out the exhaust fumes drifting up through the floorboards from the hole in the muffler.

Mutt took his eyes off the menacing M-95 potholes long enough to turn to Reino in the seat next to him. "Gawdamm, Reino, ya really look swell tonight. You figure on marryin' one a them girls at Bertha's?"

Reino was wearing his only suit, complemented by a splendid six-inch-wide necktie adorned with a large-mouth bass leaping out of the water after dragonflies. He had slathered a half pound of Clearasil on his acne. The Clearasil had set like concrete, giving him the appearance of the Joker in the *Batman* comic books.

"How come we're goin' down here on Monday night instead'a Friday or Saturday?" Reino asked.

"Too crowded on weekends," Mutt said. "We go into Davey Jones Locker on a Saturday, an' the bartender might wanna look at our driver's licenses. Too many people around to take chances servin' drinks t'minors. Monday's a dead night. They'll take any business they kin get."

"What's Davey Jones Locker?" Reino asked. "I thought we wuz goin' to Bertha's?"

"Davey Jones is a bar in Hoot Owl. Ya go there an' loosen up with a coupl'a shots. By the time we get there, you guys'll need somethin' t'take the edge off yer nerves."

"I ain't nervous . . . I'm fine," Reino said in his best John Wayne baritone as he casually kept plucking the stuffing from a hole in the Plymouth's front seat and flicking it out the window.

It was dark when we got to Hoot Owl, the trip being fairly uneventful with only one flat tire and two radiator boilovers. A huge neon sign of a 42D-cup mermaid on the roof of Davey Jones Locker beckoned to us. Mutt parked the car and turned off the ignition, but the Plymouth's engine, demonstrating its willingness to go even further, kept running for another half minute or so.

We coolly swaggered through the door. I had never been in a bar in my life, but I had seen plenty of western movies where hombres of all stripes swaggered into saloons, so I knew exactly how to do it.

Davey Jones had a heavy nautical theme: fishnet draped across the mirror in back of the bar, seashell ashtrays, captain's-chair barstools, and the like. But the most eye-catching item was the bar itself. It ran the length of the room and was a long fish tank with hundreds of tropical fish swimming around right underneath your drink. The Andrew Sisters belted out "Rum and Coca-Cola" from the Wurlitzer jukebox in the corner.

It was perfect—and it was all ours. The only other person in the place was the bartender—a big guy with a short, military haircut and tattoos on his forearms. He flashed us a friendly smile, his gold front tooth twinkling in the subdued light. "Evenin', fellas, how're things up in Michigan?"

How did he know we were from Michigan? Reino's necktie with the striking bass must have tipped him off that we were men of the great outdoors.

Mutt exchanged some good-humored banter with the bartender as we climbed onto bar stools, and I took a good look at the forest of bottles behind the bar. A thousand or more, all different shapes and sizes—I didn't know what any of them were.

"Gimme a Fox DeLuxe beer," Mutt told the bartender.

A Fox DeLuxe beer? Jeez! We drive fifty miles, and he orders a beer? I expected better from Mutt. I had to order something with a lot more class than that—but what? Then I remembered a gunslinger in one of the Randolph Scott movies. He had stood at the saloon bar—dressed in black—motionless except for his eyes scanning the room—watching everyone in the place—on the alert for one false move.

"I'll have a double shot of rye," I said, my eyes scanning the room, checking out the empty bar stools.

The bartender's eyes widened with respect. "Rye? Don't get too much call for that, but I think I gotta bottle of rye here somewhere." He dug around in the bottles at the end of the bar and pulled one out. "On the rocks or straight?"

Rocks? Is that some kind of Wisconsin custom? "Straight," I replied, playing it safe. He filled up two shot glasses and put them in front of me.

Reino was taking an entirely different tack. "So, what's good?"

The bartender placed his elbows on the fish-tank bar and leaned over towards Reino with an air of confidentiality. "Well, sir, we feature a special drink here at Davey Jones called the Mermaid's Kiss. Verrrrry smooth, but packs the punch that you Michigan men demand. Gets you up and ready for anything, know what I mean?" He gave Reino a playful punch on the shoulder that slid the bar stool back about a foot.

"Well, that sounds good t'me," Reino said. "Whomp one up."

The bartender gathered up a dozen or so bottles. He brought out an enormous glass and, jigger by jigger, started to load it up with the ingredients of the Mermaid's Kiss. I watched closely. At least three different kinds of rum went in it. Then he added more from other bottles containing strange liquids of varying viscosity and color. As each ingredient was added, the color of the Mermaid's Kiss evolved, finally taking on an iridescent, reddish-purple hue. The finishing touch was a large swizzle stick cut in the shape of a mermaid with two strategically placed prongs upon which the bartender stuck maraschino cherries.

He placed the drink on the fish-tank bar in front of Reino. The fish swimming directly below darted for safety. They had seen this engine of destruction before.

Reino took a tentative sip—paused—then a big slurp. "Gawd, this's jus' like strawberry pop." He took another healthy slug of the Mermaid's Kiss.

"Go easy on that," said the bartender. "One of those can sneak up on you."

"*One?*" Reino cried. "Sheeeet, I could put fifteen a these away." He wiped his mouth with the cuff of his suit coat. "Yeah, boy, this Hoot Owl is some nifty place."

Reino was picking up speed, and not wanting to be left behind, I picked up one of the shot glasses in front of me. As far as I knew, there was only one way to drink a shot of rye and that was gunfighter style—in one swift motion. I put the glass about two inches from my mouth and, flicking my wrist, tossed the rye in.

The result was similar to someone putting the barrel of a deer rifle between your teeth and pulling the trigger. The red-hot bullet of rye hurtled down my esophagus, performing an immediate tonsillectomy on the way in. It hit my stomach, which instantly categorized it as supremely toxic and chucked it back up. But the esophagus was having no more of it and said, "Oh, no you don't . . . it's all yours now," and shot it back down into the stomach.

Gawd, if it was this bad straight, what would it be like if you put rocks in it? I tried to tell the bartender some banal lie about how great the rye was, but my tongue and lips were totally numb, and all that came out were chimpanzee-like guttural grunts.

Fiery fumes drifted up my gullet—hairs in my nose shriveled up and dropped out on the bar. A fish below my empty shot glass stared up at me. It bore an uncanny resemblance to Clarence Hooker, our high school principal, and it was shaking its head back and forth, disapprovingly.

Instead of tossing down the second shot, I sipped it slowly, and gradually my body returned to normal. The rye had a sharp, smoky taste—not altogether unpleasant.

Meanwhile, Reino, having absorbed a lot of energy from the Mermaid's Kiss, bounded off the bar stool and over to the jukebox. He fed it a handful of nickels, and Frankie Yankovich's "Blue Skirt Waltz" whirled into the room.

Peggy Lee was next, breathing out the blues, and my pulse began to keep time with the heavy-handed bass beat.

The music was also affecting Reino's libido. Caressing the maraschino cherries on his mermaid swizzle stick, he conversed with the nearest fish below his drink, his speech sounding like a 45-rpm record played at 78. He took another big pull on his drink, and his straw sucked air at the bottom of the glass. Gently removing the cherries from the mermaid, Reino popped them in his mouth and proudly held the empty glass up to the bartender. "Gimme 'nother one a these strawberry pops."

Not to be outdone, I drained off the remains of my second shot and also held the glass up. I started thinking about Bertha's and smiled at my image in the mirror behind the bar. Damn! I never realized how much I looked like Errol Flynn—all that was missing was the mustache. I made a mental note to grow one later in the week. Reaching in my jacket pocket, I fingered the box of a dozen prophylactics. *Would that be enough?*

Mutt was still nursing his first beer. What a disappointment he was—not being able to drink like a true Michigan man.

The bartender put another Mermaid's Kiss in front of Reino and gave me two fresh shots of rye. And since we were now proven good customers, he brought out an assortment of complimentary snacks—potato chips, pretzels, a bowl of maraschino cherries for Reino, and my favorite, a jar of pickled herring. I speared a large chunk of herring and washed it down with a shot of rye. Whoops—drank it all in one swallow—it was actually pretty easy once you got the hang of it.

The evening quickly got into full swing. Reino and I were harmonizing marvelously with the Wurlitzer on "I've Got a Lovely Bunch of Coconuts," when Mutt said, "If we're goin' over to Bertha's, let's get goin'."

I climbed off the bar stool and discovered something that I hadn't noticed when we came into the bar. In keeping with the nautical theme, Davey Jones Locker was really a boat. The deck heeled sharply to port, but I instantly compensated by leaning to starboard at a forty-five-degree angle. We must be in heavy weather tonight, I thought.

Reino had his own way of dealing with the violent motion. He slid off his bar stool, dropped to the deck to lower his center of gravity, and headed for the door on his hands and knees. The gala evening must have tired him out because he suddenly decided to take a nap and pitched face down on the deck.

Mutt and the bartender picked Reino up and carried him out to the car. I followed along, glad to be on dry land again, and took a moment to watch the stars whirling around while the two of them dumped Reino in the back seat.

Mutt got behind the wheel and punched the starter, but the battery had put in a long day coming all the way down to Wisconsin. It gave one tired groan and lapsed into silence. Reaching under the seat, Mutt pulled out the crank and handed it to me. I dumbly looked at it in my hand.

"Well . . . go turn it over so we kin get 'er started," Mutt said. "I'll work the gas pedal. Yer too fried to do that right."

I reeled over to the front of the car and, after seven or eight pokes, got the crank engaged to the Plymouth's engine. I straddled the front bumper and started to crank the engine.

The Plymouth had been slumbering contentedly in front of Davey Jones Locker for two hours and deeply resented the intrusion of the crank. It maliciously fired one cylinder, violently backlashing the crank in my hand and bending my right thumb back one-hundred-and-eighty degrees from its normal operating position. I fell backwards over the bumper into an icy puddle of slush, cursing and shaking my misaligned thumb in the air.

Mutt stuck his head out of the car window. "Quitcher bitchin'. It ain't yer thumb yer gonna be usin' over at Bertha's."

We finally got the car started and took off. All that exercise had mobilized the unstable mixture of rye and pickled herring, triggering off violent eruptions in my sinus cavities and tear ducts. Reino snored peacefully in the back seat. Judging by the rum fumes permeating the car and the maraschino-red bubbles he was blowing in his sleep, it was clear that he wasn't going to participate in any further activities that night.

Bertha's was an unobtrusive, cinder-block building on the other side of town. Over the entrance an ancient neon sign flickered "BEER." Mutt wisely decided to leave the Plymouth's engine running since the battery was on its last legs. We entered what appeared to be another bar but one far less elegant than Davey Jones Locker. In the dim light, unoccupied, cheap formica-topped tables circled a small dance floor where two women were dancing together—an Eddy Arnold love song crooned on the jukebox. There were six women and a gray-haired bartender in the place.

One of the women had been watching us through dirty venetian blinds on the front window when we pulled into the parking lot. There wasn't any doubt that she was in charge.

"You boys must *real-ly* be lonesome, just leavin' the engine runnin' like that," Bertha said with a cement-mixer-like chortle. She could have been mistaken for Ma Kettle except for her copper-colored, tightly curled hair and savagely purple dress, drum-tight on her large, buxom frame. Bertha took a couple of puffs on a rum-soaked crook cigar and blew smoke in our direction. The pickled herring in my gut toyed with the idea of swimming upstream.

Mutt didn't waste any time on small talk, but made a beeline for one of the women—a small blonde and by far the best-looking woman in the place. They exchanged a few words and slipped through a curtain at the back of the room.

I was left standing alone by the door, paralyzed by fear and indecision, slush dripping off my mackinaw. But Bertha charged up and buckled my knees with a beefy arm thrown across my shoulders. "Why don'cha lemme introduce ya to a nice young lady." She put a vice-like grip on my arm and marched me toward three women sitting at a small table. I looked around frantically for the one that looked like Mildred Spagarelli, as Mutt had promised. I didn't spot her, but one of them *did* look a little like Mildred's mother—in fact, *all* of them looked like someone's mother.

Bertha leaned over and croaked in my ear. "This ain't exactly the varsity squad I got on tonight, being as how Mondays're dead an' the reg'lar girls take the day off, but I'm gonna introduce ya to a real sweetheart." We got to the table, and as if by a prearranged signal, two of the three women got up and left.

This here's Ginger," Bertha announced, pulling out a chair. "Why don'cha sit down an' get t'know her." Bertha left and I sat down.

Ginger sized me up like a black widow spider that had just snared a fat fly in her web. With her upswept hair, she looked a little like Betty Grable except with a whole lot more mileage. Her sequined, low-cut red dress was held up by two narrow straps, straining to keep her industrial-sized bosom in check. She slowly crossed her legs, exposing two square yards of thigh, and gave me a Cheshire-cat smile. "Wanna buy me a drink?"

"Well . . . sure . . . sure . . . what would you like to drrr . . . "

Ginger had already signalled the bartender who whipped out a full drink from underneath the bar, put it on a tray, and brought it over. "That'll be two dollars," he said to me, placing the drink in front of her.

Jeez . . . two dollars for a drink! Still, you couldn't complain about the service. If the drinks had been served that quick over at Davey Jones Locker, I'd be in a coma and Reino would be dead. I pulled out two dollar bills and gave them to the bartender. "Ya want somethin' from the bar, too?" he asked.

"Uh : . . no, thanks." Booze was the furthest thing from my mind right then. The rye was wearing off and my throbbing head was in a full-fledged domestic squabble with my stomach. I just wanted to get rid of my virginity and go home to bed.

I didn't know what to do next, and we just sat there looking at each other for a few moments. Finally, Ginger said, "Why don't we go to my room in the back where we can have a little privacy?" She picked up her two-dollar drink and stood.

This is it. I took a ragged breath and followed her through the curtain into a long, narrow hallway that reeked of stale beer, cigarette smoke, and other things that eluded identification. She stopped at a door, rapped on it lightly, waited for a second, and opened it.

The room had a double bed with a richly stained chenille bedspread, a night stand, one chair, and that was it. Ginger walked over to the bed and turned to me. I stood paralyzed in the doorway.

I stood paralyzed in the doorway.

"Come on in . . . it's okay," she said soothingly. She sat down on the bed and patted a place next to her, motioning for me to sit down. Again, we just looked at each other for a second. Then, to show that I wasn't a complete mental defective at making small talk, I said, "I guess we'll need these," and brought out the box of a dozen prophylactics.

Her eyes widened. She reached in the front of her dress and pulled out a single packet. "I figure that one might do the job." Then she added, "You gotta pay me first, ya know."

"Oh . . . yeah . . . yeah . . . I know." I took out my wallet and reached inside. One dollar. *One dollar?* In a panic, I searched through all my pockets. Nothing. The festivities over at Davey Jones Locker had taken a devastating monetary toll.

I shot her a desperate look. "I guess it's more'n I got left, huh?"

She barked a quick laugh. "Just a bit. You ain't done this before, have ya?"

"No," I said in a small, quiet voice.

She got up from the bed, lit up another cigarette, and stood there facing the wall, cupping her elbow, and tapping one shoe on the floor. "Chrissake, I *told* Bertha not to set me up with first-timers."

"She didn't know," I said quickly. Suddenly, the full impact of my sorry financial state dawned on me. "Jeez, I'll never hear the end of it when the guys get wind of this." I got up from the bed and the room listed sharply to port again. I braced myself against the wall. I was getting tired of sailing with the Wisconsin Navy.

"You okay?"

"I gotta bad headache."

She reached in her purse and brought out a tin of aspirins. She shook out two and handed them to me along with the drink she'd carried in from the bar. "Here . . . take these."

"I can't wash 'em down with that drink. I've had enough tonight."

"It's only iced tea . . . won't hurt you."

"Iced tea?" *Two dollars for iced tea?*

She smiled. "Whoops . . . I wasn't supposed to let that out. That's one of Bertha's main sources of income."

I swallowed the aspirin and took a sip of the tea. It tasted better than anything else I'd had that night. I took a big gulp—what the hell—I paid two dollars for it.

Ginger picked up her purse and edged toward the door. "Means a lot to you . . . what the guys think . . . don't it?"

I handed the tea back. "I guess so."

"Lemme tell ya somethin' . . . runnin' outta money tonight is probably the bes' thing that could've happened to you. You may wind up havin' a hundred girl friends or get married five times, but you'll never forget the *first* time, and you oughta make it one of the *best* times. Forget about places like this. Whaddarya? Fifteen . . . sixteen? Ya got plenty a time. Kids always think they gotta grow up inna hurry. Take it from me . . . growin' up ain't all it's cracked up to be."

She lifted her skirt, peeled off a fancy, black garter from her leg, and handed it to me. "As for your friends . . . show 'em this, an' tell 'em you had a helluva good time."

"Why are ya doin' this?"

She opened the door. "Beats the hell outta me . . . it's terrible for bus'ness."

Mutt fingered the black garter in the dim light of the Plymouth's instrument panel as we headed north. He whistled appreciatively. "She gave you this, huh?"

"Yeah."

"Must'a really liked ya. None of 'em ever give me one a these. Wanna go again in a coupla weeks?"

I stared out at the dark spruce trees drifting past the window. The patches of snow among the trees were gone now. The baseball diamond would probably be dried out in a week or two.

"No," I replied.

The Last Waltz

*T*obacco juice leaked from the corner of Carl Kettu's mouth as he slowly circled the pool table, totally engrossed in surveying the layout of the striped balls—looking for his best shot. The juice picked up speed, coursed down his chin and neck, and disappeared into his woolen shirt. I took an unconscious swipe across my own chin.

Store-bought cigarettes were too expensive, and Carl had already incinerated his eyebrows lighting up a loosely packed roll-your-own. Nevertheless, he seemed determined on picking up the nicotine habit since he was now experimenting with Peerless chewing tobacco.

April 1949—it was a gray, drizzly Saturday afternoon in our small Upper Michigan town of Republic. Carl and I were locked in a high-stakes game of eightball at Stumpy Bercanelli's Pool Hall in the basement below Anderson's Hardware Store, fighting it out to see who would buy the next round of Nesbitt's Orange soda pop.

I chalked up my cue stick, awaiting my turn. "Ya ask a girl to the prom yet?"

Carl selected a tricky double-bank shot designed to put the fourteen ball in the side pocket. "Naw, not yet. No sweat, though. There's plenty of 'em waitin' fer me t'ask 'em. How 'bout you?"

"Me neither. I just been lookin' the girls over, so far."

"Who ya got it narrowed down to?" Carl asked.

"Well . . . I'm thinkin' of askin' Mildred Spagarelli." Mildred was a sultry, curly haired, freshman beauty whose ripening body was making old man Spagarelli very nervous.

Carl chuckled dryly. "You serious? Bet'cha any amount a money Petersen's takin' her." Carl Petersen, the center on our varsity basketball team, was the ranking member of our high-school aristocracy. It was well known that he could get any girl to dump her current heartthrob with the twitch of an eyebrow.

"Anyway," Carl continued, "we got a more serious problem than figurin' out what girls t'take. Where we gonna get a car?" At this embryonic stage of our exploits with the opposite sex, Carl and I always went as a twosome for moral support.

"How about yer old man's truck?"

"Hah!" Carl exclaimed, spraying tobacco juice in all directions. "This is the Junior Prom, dummy. Kin you see four of us . . . the girls in them big, fluffy gowns . . . crammed in the seat of that pickup truck? B'sides, if we wanna take 'em someplace fancy afterward . . . down the road to Marquette or Ishpeming . . . we need sumthin' classier than that truck."

Old man Kettu's '41 Ford pickup truck was the only weapon at our disposal whenever Carl and I waged our guerrilla-warfare courting on the town's teen-age females. Our tactics were direct: we drove slowly around town, then swooped down on a pair of seemingly unsuspecting girls and tried to charm them into riding around with us.

The fact that we ever got *any* girls at all into Kettu's pickup was incredible in itself. The truck's engine was never firing on more than three cylinders at a time and belched huge clouds of bilious blue smoke as it loudly backfired. The cab exuded a pungent fragrance, contributed largely by Kettu's dog, Fart, an aptly named, extremely unbathed animal who liked to ride everywhere with old man Kettu.

All this tended to put a damper on whatever romantic inclinations the girls may have had. However, it was a moot point. With four people crammed in like sardines, there was zero maneuvering room in the cab for any amorous moves. It was okay though—Carl and I were generally satisfied with close female body contact.

"I might be able to talk my Uncle Arne into letting me use his '36 Chevy," I volunteered. "I'll get my driver's license just in time for the prom."

Carl's eyes gleamed. "*Now* yer talkin'. You do the drivin' fer a change, an' I get the back seat with my girl." Another rivulet of tobacco juice squirmed out of his mouth as he gripped down on the Peerless with his back teeth, while he imagined the possibilities of several hours in the back seat with the girl of his choice. Distracted by lust, he missed his double-bank shot.

It was my turn, and I was mentally going through the physics of a four-ball combination shot when the poolroom grew silent—Alice Maki had come in.

Stumpy Bercanelli's Pool Hall was a male stronghold, and females weren't welcome. All the guys stared at her with open hostility.

"MA SEZ FOR YOU T'COME HOME," Alice yelled at her younger brother, Piggy, who was across the room at Table Three, shooting a game of rotation with some of his pals.

This was the worst possible thing a woman could do to a guy—giving him orders in front of his friends. Piggy knew this and responded accordingly.

"KISS MY BUTT," he yelled back.

Without hesitation, Alice bounded over to the wall and snatched a pool cue from the rack. Gripping it firmly by the small end and waggling it like a baseball bat, she advanced quickly on her brother. Carl and I hastily stepped back out of harm's way. Piggy's confidence evaporated, and he bolted for the door. Slamming the cue back in the rack, Alice followed him out.

I watched the scene with immense interest, admiring the way she handled the situation. I knew Alice very well. As kids, we had frittered away many happy hours engaged in typical Upper Michigan juvenile pursuits. But about a year ago, for no good reason, she decided that it was not socially acceptable for a young lady to be skinning weasels and shooting rats at the town dump. Since then we'd only had a few brief encounters.

But Providence must have put Alice here at this very moment, I thought. Time-critical decisions had to be made about the prom. The need of the moment overcame my normally cool demeanor, and I impulsively charged out after her.

"Uh . . . hi, Alice. Say . . . I wuz wonderin' . . . has anybody asked you to the Junior Prom yet?"

"What's it to ya?"

Puberty obviously wasn't agreeing with her, but I continued on in a soothing voice. "Well . . . I wuz jus' thinkin' that if you weren't going with anybody else, that . . . maybe you an' I might go . . . with each other, I mean."

Her surly expression softened a little. "That's on a Saturday night, and I always listen to 'Your Hit Parade' on the radio."

"Yeah, that's my favorite program, too, an' I really hate to miss it, but everybody expects ya to go to the prom . . . you know how it is . . . "

She thought for a few seconds. "Well . . . what the heck . . . I like to dance . . . why not?"

My heart did a little flutter. *She accepted!* It must have been my smooth approach.

"You *do* know how to dance, don't you?" Alice asked.

"Dance? Oh . . . yeah . . . sure . . . heh, heh. I *love* to dance . . . heh, heh." I hurried back into the pool hall to confer with Carl.

"Now, pay attention," Mrs. Kettu commanded while facing me. "Take one step toward me with yer left foot." Carl and I had raced over to his house from the pool hall seeking emergency dance lessons from his mother, Dagmar.

I hesitated a moment too long, and she grabbed my left thigh, yanked my leg forward, and planted it firmly on the floor. "Now, bring your right foot forward, too, but swing it around in an L and put it down over here." She put a hand behind my right knee and wrenched that leg into position. "Now, put your left foot over next to the right one, and you're ready to do the whole thing backwards."

After a couple of runs through the pattern, she strode over to the old Victrola and wound it up with the crank. The huge shiny arm containing the needle plopped down on the 78-rpm record, and strains of "The Skater's Waltz" wobbled tinnily from the huge morning-glory-shaped speaker. The scratches on the record added a nice realistic touch—like skate blades cutting along the ice.

Mrs. Kettu grabbed my left hand and jerked my arm up to shoulder height, coming within a whisker of dislocating my shoulder. "This's where you hold yer left hand. Now, put yer other hand on my waist."

I reached out for her boiler-sized waist, but didn't have a prayer of making it without brushing up against her mammoth bosom—like trying to wrap your arms around the front end of a Buick without touching the grill.

I struggled with this embarrassing dilemma for several seconds. Finally, she reeled me in and mashed my breastbone into the EE cups of her Gossard corset. "C'mon . . . c'mon, we ain't got all day. I gotta cook supper."

I clumped around drunkenly in a two-foot-square area, trying in vain to synchronize my footfalls with the tempo of "The Skater's Waltz." "Relax," she said. "Try t'drift along with the music. Just pretend we're skating across a lake in the moonlight."

*She reeled me in and mashed my breastbone into
the EE cups of her Gossard corset.*

"Better hope the ice is pretty thick if yer skatin' with my mom," Carl added from the sideline.

Mrs. Kettu dropped my left hand. "Okay, *Mister* Fred Astaire," she snapped at Carl. "Yer next."

Following the dance lesson, I was in a state of high excitement as I hurried home. I had never been on a *real date* where I actually invited the girl beforehand, got all dressed up, and took her to some public place. My brain simmered with the logistics.

My mother was standing on a couple of two-by-eights spanning a pair of sawhorses as she scrubbed the living-room ceiling—a quaint house-cleaning custom that Finnish women faithfully observed every spring.

"Ma, I need a new suit," I announced.

The statement jolted her, and she struggled for balance, swaying precariously on the boards. Every August she dragged me down to J. C. Penney's to try on new clothes for the coming school year. Now, for me to come forward, of my own accord, and state that *I need a new suit*—that was too much.

"I wasn't going to get you a new suit until high-school graduation," she said. "That's two years away."

"I'm gonna take Alice Maki to the Junior Prom."

"Junior Prom?"

"It's a big dance in the high school gym. You invite a girl, get all dressed up in a suit, white shirt, an' tie, buy the girl a cor . . . a cor . . . a flower, an' afterward, you take her someplace fancy to eat."

"Fancy? There aren't any fancy places t'eat in this town."

"I know, I know. I'm gonna ask Arne if I can borrow his car an' drive to Ishpeming or Marquette."

"Ishpeming? That's over twenty miles! Drive? You don't even have a driver's license."

"I'll have it in time for the prom, and I been practicing my driving a lot with Arvid's jeep."

Neither of my parents knew how to drive, so we didn't own a car. Having driven teams of horses in an earlier career as a lumber-camp teamster, my old man was firmly convinced that horses had more sense than automobile drivers; consequently, he rode in mechanized vehicles *only* when absolutely necessary. As a good Lutheran, my mother knew that only *fast* women drove cars.

My uncle Arvid (Arne's brother) had taken it upon himself to teach me to drive. He had an elegant '47 Chevy, but I wasn't allowed to touch it, lest I dent a fender. Instead, I logged in my driving lessons in a 1943 Dodge command car that Arvid had picked up at a war-surplus auction. The Dodge was undentable—a powerful, overgrown Jeep with a thick, steel-plate chassis made to deflect Nazi machine-gun bullets. The transmission alone weighed two thousand pounds, and you double-clutched to shift gears. Still in all, I was progressing very nicely, only knocking down an occasional tree around the township's back roads. I could easily become an urban driver with a few days' practice.

During supper we were still discussing the details of the Junior Prom.

"Alice Maki . . . ain't she the one that used to pound up on you?" the old man asked, as he pushed hash onto his fork with a piece of home-baked bread.

"That wuz a long time ago . . . we were just kids," I replied defensively.

"I'm going to go with you to pick out the suit," my mother stated. "I want to make sure it's big enough so it'll still fit you for graduation."

"So what's all this gonna cost ya?" the old man asked, making it perfectly clear he wasn't going to be involved in financing this operation.

"Well," I said, "the flowers, gas, and food will probably run close to twenty dollars . . . plus the suit."

He gawked at me in disbelief. "*Twenty dollars?* I never spent that much the whole time yer mother an' I wuz goin' together before we got married."

"That's true," my mother admitted. "It wasn't a cent over ten dollars."

The next Monday, Carl and I slogged home from school through the springtime mud.

"Boy, that Alice's got some mean streak in her," Carl remarked as he recounted Saturday's near-brawl in the pool hall. "Too bad . . . she'll flatten ya if you try anything funny on prom night."

"Look, at least I *got* a date. When you gonna get around to askin' somebody?"

"Oh, I did that this afternoon," he replied offhandedly.

"Who?"

"Martha Furgus."

"*Martha Furgus*?" I blurted out. The news startled me. Martha was a junior, but dwelt on the fringes of our high-school society. As a matter of fact, I couldn't remember ever saying anything to her. A skinny, mousy girl, she kept pretty much to herself. She seemed to be some kind of chemistry whiz, spending a lot of time in the science lab where she had a part-time job cleaning test tubes or something. I recalled passing her in the hall one day and detecting a strong chemical odor. Her clothes had small, brown holes eaten in them.

"Yeah, well . . . she's nice'n quiet," I said lamely.

"That's right," Carl replied quickly. "An' I always liked older women."

The final days before the prom were busy with preparations. My mother and I made a clothes-buying trek to J. C. Penney's in Ishpeming. Reasoning that a growing boy was sure to gain at least seventy-five pounds before graduation, she picked out a royal-blue, gabardine suit that would fit a buffalo.

My Uncle Arne closely inspected my driver's license and grudgingly consented to let me borrow his '36 Chevy. Arne wasn't much of a hand at keeping an automobile clean, so the day before the prom, Carl and I picked up the car and got down to business. We hosed off the winter's accumulation of hard-caked mud and applied several coats of Johnson's Wax till the rusted fenders gleamed luxuriously in the sunlight. We meticulously groomed the inside. Carl swept the frayed upholstery with a whisk broom while I scoured and waxed the steering wheel and instrument panel. We threw the floor mats over the clothesline and beat out every speck of dust.

It was absolutely essential that the car be in pristine condition—we were going to the Mather Inn in Ishpeming for a late-night supper after the prom. The Mather Inn—the fanciest eatery in Marquette County—would put a serious dent in our finances, but Carl and I were totally caught up in the moment, and no expense would be spared.

By mid-afternoon on Saturday, the wood stove in Kettu's sauna was glowing. Gallons of water were thrown on the hot rocks and the temperature soared. Stripped down, Carl and I climbed to the top bench to thoroughly flush out our adolescent poisons.

Back at home I trotted out my brand-new Gillette safety razor and scraped off the five neophyte whiskers protruding from my chin. Each pimple was soaked with a hot washcloth and liberally coated with Clearasil.

I removed the cellophane and price tags from the new underwear and began the lengthy process of getting dressed. The heavy starch in my only white shirt made it necessary to punch my arms through the sealed sleeves to get it on. I carefully put a slip knot in one of my prized possessions—a sky-blue necktie with a formation of B-17 Flying Fortresses in flight across the six-inch-wide rayon material.

Ironing-board-size lapels on the suit coat nicely complemented its mammoth shoulders. The waistline of the pants bunched up severely when I ratcheted the belt to my twenty-eight-inch waist, but this was barely discernible with the coat on.

With the aid of a shoehorn, I crammed my feet into the granite-like leather of a new pair of shoes.

Lastly, I tackled my hair. A daunting task, but I had carefully refined the procedure over the past month. I blended in several ounces of Wildroot Creme Oil and kneaded the hair into a bread-dough-like texture. With a comb I expertly sculpted a towering wave that leaned out over my forehead like the surf at Hawaii's Banzai Pipeline.

I was finished. Inspecting myself closely in my mother's full-length mirror, I realized that Alice Maki wouldn't be in my league tonight. I needed Ginger Rogers.

I drove the Chevy over to Carl's house and leaned on the horn impatiently. Carl hurried out carrying a corsage. I was immediately envious—he had a hair wave even higher than mine.

Minutes later we picked up Martha Furgus. She looked much better than usual. How could I have missed the fact that she had developed such a nifty figure? Carl noticed the same thing and laughed nervously as he helped her into the back seat.

We drove over to pick up Alice. At first I didn't recognize her. She was all decked out in a baby-blue chiffon, ankle-length gown. Her hair, usually wound up in a tight bun, now floated around her face in saucy curls. Her freckles had magically disappeared. Her eyelashes had grown half an inch. She was ravishing. There was a strong possibility that before the evening was over I'd be hopelessly in love.

The Chevy's engine purred contentedly as we drove to the school. The evening showed great promise—the mud puddles on the dirt roads were drying up and the few isolated rain clouds were well away on the horizon. I modestly displayed my driving skills, smoothly double-clutching through the gears, weaving only occasionally.

From all over the township, brilliantly waxed cars converged on the school, bearing lovely, masterfully coiffured girls in glorious evening dress and clean-shaven, dashing young men with rigid pompadours soaring into the evening sky.

The theme of this year's Junior Prom was "Springtime in Michigan." The inside of the gymnasium had been cleverly and painstakingly transformed into a woodland paradise. Strategically placed five-cell flashlights created a subdued lighting that highlighted crepe-paper streamers strung from the walls to the center of the ceiling. Green paper ferns dotted the sidelines. Dozens of colorful cloth-covered card tables were aligned along the walls. On each table sat a cheerful wooden beaver resting on his flat tail, artfully cut from one-inch pine stock in the woodshop. Each beaver clutched a Mason jar full of forget-me-nots and pussy willows. Even the metal tubing on the folding chairs was festively decorated with green paper vines.

"Pretty nice, eh?" Carl said, as we selected a table. We all agreed.

The Junior Prom was the one occasion during the year when a *real live orchestra* came to town. This year Frankie Dominic and his Collegiate Wolverines were on hand to provide the dance music. The four of them, nattily attired in lilac sports coats and violet slacks, blended in smoothly with the springtime theme. As we were getting settled, Frankie picked up his immense, gleaming accordion and magically rippled into the introduction of "Mockin' Bird Hill."

I hastily reviewed Dagmar Kettu's dance instructions in my mind as Alice and I walked onto the basketball floor. We lurched off in my box step, carving out little squares at the free-throw line. Every fourth beat or so, I tromped smartly on Alice's toes, but she didn't complain. I was doing quite well, actually, counting out the tempo: *one*—two—three, *one*—two—three. When Alice gave me a pained look, I realized I was counting aloud. I immediately reduced it to small, almost-inaudible grunts.

One of the Wolverines put down his clarinet and began crooning the lyrics to "The Tennessee Waltz"—better to dance to than "Mockin' Bird Hill" because it was slower, with a distinct downbeat friendly to the box step. The floor filled up—other guys guiding their dates around their own little squares. Not too bad, I thought, relaxing in the anonymity of the crowd. Alice cleverly adjusted to my dancing style, and I squashed her foot only now and then.

I DON' WAN' 'ER, YOU CAN HAVE 'ER, SHE'S TOO
FAT FOR ME . . .

Without warning, the Collegiate Wolverines began belting out the "Too Fat Polka." It was one of my favorite songs, but something started to go terribly wrong. The dancers were moving faster and hopping around a lot. I sped up my *one*—two—three, *one*—two—three but couldn't seem to catch up. Mrs. Kettu, a devout waltz enthusiast, had failed to mention that there was a basic difference between waltzes and polkas—*tempo*. Of course, I didn't know this at the time, so I zealously shifted my box step into overdrive, dazzling the other dancers with my amazing footwork.

Alice knew all about polka dancing and wasn't too happy with my innovative approach. She told me she wanted to sit down.

"I thought you knew how to dance," she said irritably.

"Well . . . I really prefer the slow, romantic ones."

She folded her arms across her chest, clearly miffed. "Well, the songs aren't *all* slow and romantic. I suppose we'll just have to sit out some of them."

As if demonstrating her point, Frankie Dominic began bellowing out "Mule Train." I flinched every time the drummer stood up and cracked his authentic-looking mule-skinner whip, praying that Alice wouldn't want to get me out on the floor.

Carl, a graduate of the same dance school, was having as much trouble as I was, so we excused ourselves to discuss strategy at the refreshment table.

"It's simple," Carl said under his breath as he filled two cups with some nondescript reddish liquid from the punch bowl. "We bribe the band."

It was a brilliant plan. We sidled over to Frankie Dominic and covertly slipped him three dollars to play slow numbers like "The Tennessee Waltz" at every opportunity. Frankie smiled knowingly and pocketed the money.

Sure enough, a few minutes later the band began playing "The Tennessee Waltz" again. I unhesitatingly led Alice out to the dance floor.

After it had been played for the third time, I had memorized the lyrics and crooned them softly in Alice's ear, my voice fluctuating back and forth between soprano and baritone, as it had a habit of doing.

"I'm really starting to hate this song," Alice rasped during the fifth "Tennessee Waltz," her fingernails digging painfully into my shoulder each time I crushed her foot. When the band took an intermission, Alice breathed a sigh of relief and went off with Martha to powder their noses. Carl and I went back to the refreshment table, congratulating ourselves on our cleverness.

Mutt Hukala was bellied up to the punch bowl. I could tell at a glance, just by the way he was standing there, he was up to something.

A paper bag was concealed under his coat, and the mouth of an open bottle was peeking out of the bag—Mutt holding it just over the rim of the punch bowl. A colorless liquid glugged into the punch.

"I think this shindig needs a little livening up, don't you?" Mutt murmured conspiringly.

"What *is* that?" I whispered.

"Vodka," he replied. "Can't taste it, but I bet'cha it'll loosen up sum a these prim little dollies." He emptied the quart bottle into the punch.

This was a bold stunt. The gym floor was constantly being patrolled by a large squad of grim-faced chaperons—teachers from all grades called up for duty to keep the students from committing unspeakable, immoral acts like dancing too close.

"Here, lemme try some of that," Carl said. He ladled some punch into a paper cup and took a swig, then smacked his lips and grinned wickedly. "Damn . . . yer right. Ya can't taste a thing except that fruity crap. I'm gonna take sum back to the table for Martha, heh, heh."

I thought about that for a moment, but then the image of Alice waving the cue in the pool hall flashed into my mind. What would she do if she had a snootful? I played it safe with two ten-cent Coca-Colas.

The band opened the second half with a lengthy series of three-quarter-time numbers, and Alice and I dutifully box-stepped into the late evening hours. By now, the new shoes felt like they were riveted to my feet. My once-crisp shirt was limp with perspiration, but the collar remained stiff, gnawing into my skin like a cross-cut saw blade. The horde of sweating bodies on the dance floor sent the gymnasium temperature soaring.

Alice was faring no better. Her curly hair was unwinding like a tired clock spring. Freckles were emerging through the rapidly melting layer of makeup on her flushed cheeks, and one eye had eyelashes an inch longer than the other. Not surprisingly, she had a serious limp from the constant punishment of being stepped on.

Just when we had reached our limit of pain and suffering, Frankie Dominic, in the midst of the tenth rendition of "The Tennessee Waltz," dropped his accordion on the floor. It seemed that Frankie had been liberally sampling the punch during the band intermissions and hadn't secured the straps firmly when they began this set. Odd-looking accordion pieces rolled around the floor. Fortunately, Mr. Troutman, our high-school biology teacher, having become fast friends with the band members over by the punch bowl, immediately took charge. He declared that anyone who was qualified to teach frog dissection could certainly put an accordion back together.

Carl doggedly kept plying Martha with the spiked punch while we sat at the table. The vodka finally began to dissolve her sedate personality.

"You want me to recite the periodic table?" she said. Her eyes glowed in the dim light.

Carl, who had been sneaking his arm across the top of the back of her chair, paused. "What?"

"The periodic table . . . I can recite the whole thing."

"What's a periodic table?"

Martha took another snort of punch. "The periodic table of elements, silly. You'll get it in chemistry class next year."

Carl didn't reply. This was not going the way he intended. Chemistry was not a subject that had come up in any dates he had previously been on.

"Bet'cha can't do it without making a mistake," Alice challenged, ready to listen to anything to stay off her feet.

Martha shut her eyes. "Here goes . . . hydrogen, helium, lithium, beryllium . . . "

Miss Tilley, the third-grade teacher, approached with a glass of punch in each hand. She wobbled to a stop at our table and cast an owlish glare at Carl.

"Amazing."

"What's that, Miz Tilley?" Carl asked politely, pulling his attention away from Martha.

"That you're still in school. 'That Kettu kid's a half-wit,' I told Superintendent Schuyler many years ago. 'He'll never make it through the sixth grade,' I said to him. Well . . . I guess I was wrong . . . here you are . . . two years away from graduation. My, my, our school system must be going to hell."

Carl didn't say anything.

"Arsenic, selenium, bromine, krypton . . . " Martha chanted, eyes closed.

"Didn't know we were still teaching Latin in high school," Miss Tilley said. She stared blearily at Alice. "And who might you be, my dear?"

"Why, Miss Tilley, don't you recognize me? I'm Alice Maki."

"The hell you say! Goodness, you've changed. I always said that it was too bad you weren't a boy. I remember the time you coldcocked Tommy Nardi on the playground during recess. You really had a wicked left hook in those days, although I'm no judge of things like that."

Alice clenched her teeth, her face turning a deep crimson.

This was bad. In a matter of seconds I would be in the cross hairs of Miss Tilley's candid personal evaluations. Worse, Frankie Dominic might get his accordion back together at any moment, and I would be doomed to another hour or two of dancing—my feet screamed silently at the thought.

The solution presented itself when a menacing rumble drifted up from my stomach. It hadn't seen food in a long time. I quickly stood up.

"Gee, Miss Tilley," I said in a loud voice to drown out my stomach. "It's been real nice talking to you, but we have to get going."

A late-night supper at the Mather Inn had now become a matter of survival since no one had eaten anything since lunch. As we sped into the night, northbound on M-95, Carl, Alice, and I passed the time fantasizing over menu selections. Martha, who had mentally stalled out at neodymium, sat silently in the back seat, desperately rummaging her memory for the next element.

My mood was improving. What could possibly go wrong from here on? After all, I already had plenty of experience eating.

Suddenly, steam began pouring out of the front of the Chevy. I pulled off the road, unlatched the hood, and peered in. The radiator was angrily spewing water and steam through a hole in the core.

"What'll we do?" said Alice, gazing gloomily around at the blackness of the nearby woods.

"I dunno," I muttered. It was a terrible place to break down—six or seven miles out of Republic and a long way from Ishpeming. To make matters worse, we didn't have any spare water with us—a cardinal sin of omission.

While we were standing morosely by the front of the car, a bobbing light appeared in the trees. A dark form emerged from the woods, weaving its way toward us, carrying a flashlight.

"Hey there," a gravelly voice boomed out. "Ya got trouble, eh?"

It was Buckshot Jarvi—one of several old Finn guys living in camps out in the woods, working only when extreme economic duress made it necessary.

Buckshot flashed his light quickly over our faces, then stuck his head under the hood and played the flashlight beam on the radiator core. "Got a purty good-sized hole in 'er. Prob'ly caught a rock from a passin' car."

"Where did *you* come from?" Carl asked.

"Gotta camp jus' off th'road over there." Buckshot waved the beam at the dark woods. "Heard ya when ya got outta th'car. Glad y'stopped by," he added cordially. "Ain't talked t'nobody in damn near a week." He stared with curiosity at the girls' formal gowns.

"You got any water?" I asked. "We're on our way to Ishpeming."

Buckshot lifted his dirty wool hunting cap and scratched his head. "Car ain't gonna get to Ishpeming with a hole like that in th'radiator. I got water. Ya kin fill 'er up, an' it might get ya back to Republic, but that's about it. I wouldn't try nuthin' further than that 'fore ya get 'er fixed."

"But we were going to eat at the Mather Inn," Alice wailed.

Buckshot was impressed. "Izzat so? Ain't never been in the place, m'self. Understand some a them dinners goes as high as four or five dollars. Hell, I don' spend that much fer grub in a week."

"If I had any idea that something like this might happen, I would have eaten supper at home," Alice muttered.

"Y'mean t'say you kids ain't had *supper* yet?" Buckshot thundered. "Tha's no problem. I got plenty a grub. We'll get sumthin' in yer gut right now."

Alice's voice shot up an octave. "No . . . no . . . I can wait till we get home."

Buckshot wasn't going to take no for an answer. "C'mon!" he commanded, motioning violently with his arm toward the woods. "No trouble at all. B'sides, ya ain't goin' nowheres 'til that engine block cools down, an' you kids don' wanna stay out here in the cold, do ya?"

We reluctantly stumbled after him into the dark woods. There was a footpath through dense undergrowth that meandered about a hundred yards to a small log cabin. Dim light filtered out through dust-caked panes of a single window. Buckshot pushed open a tar-paper-covered door and marched inside. We trooped in behind him.

When the five of us got inside the one room, we were standing cheek by jowl. A rickety, oilcloth-covered table, holding a slew of empty Fox DeLuxe beer bottles, sat in the center of the pine-plank floor. A kerosene lamp on an upended orange crate cast feeble light on the log walls. A large, dark cat—or at least what I *hoped* was a cat—darted across the floor and into the shadows.

Carl's forehead smacked into a well-populated ribbon of fly paper hanging from the rafters. The sticky substance grabbed onto his hair, leaving his well-sculpted wave in utter ruin.

With a practiced motion, Buckshot scooped up the empty beer bottles from the table with one arm and dropped them in a corner with a crash. He positioned the empty table near the edge of his bunk bed.

"Only got two chairs, so you two guys sit on the bunk and give the young ladies th'good seats."

Carl and I sank deep into the bunk bed, a thin pallet piled high with old, woolen army blankets, supported only by sagging webbing. Our chins barely came up to the top of the table.

Buckshot scurried around, obviously pleased to have such elegant company. He immediately strode over to the cast-iron stove, opened up one of the lids and heaved a couple of maple logs on top of glowing embers. Dented pie tins were placed on the oilcloth in front of us. In no time he had leftover stew, a large pot of coffee, and a frying pan full of eggs cooking merrily on the stove.

The stove blasted out heat, and rivers of sweat gushed forth from my armpits and ran down my rib cage. I peeled off my suit coat and noticed a thick, black greasy streak trailing down one sleeve. My pant legs were soaked from the wet ferns along the path, and a fuzzy, brown caterpillar was crawling up the laces of one of my now-scuffed shoes, intent on exploring my leg.

Martha, who hadn't uttered a word since we stopped the car, sat bolt upright. Her face cleared up with recall. "Aha! Promethium!"

Buckshot paused as he put down pieces of hardtack next to each of the pie tins. "A foreign girl, eh? Where's she from . . . Italy? . . . Greece?"

"Samarium, europium, gadolinium, terbium . . ."

"I guess she don't speak much English, does she?" Buckshot said.

The food was ready. From the pot, Buckshot ladled out generous portions of steaming mojakka into the pie tins. Mojakka, a Finnish stew that we were all too familiar with, consisted of boiled potatoes, carrots, celery, onions, and beef—although the gamy fragrance suggested some kind of meat other than beef.

We stared at the mojakka in dismay. Our empty stomachs and frustrated plans were in a monumental struggle.

Buckshot gently placed a fried egg on top of each portion of stew. The edges of the egg were scorched jet-black, and the broken yellow yolks were trickling into the thick brown stew.

He stepped back to admire his handiwork. "Kind'a colorful, ain't it?" he declared modestly, wiping his hands on a red bandanna. "Now, dig right in! You'll never see nuthin' like this at the Mather Inn, will ya? Heh, heh."

We quickly shook our heads in agreement and obediently picked up our forks.

An hour later we were driving back to Republic. It was still dark, but heavy rain clouds were visibly lurking above us, threatening a soggy morning.

It was a very quiet ride back. No one had anything they wanted to discuss in public. Alice closed her eyes and leaned her head up against the passenger-side window, but I knew she wasn't sleeping. I softly played the Motorola radio mounted underneath the dash, hoping it might dilute the wretchedness of the evening's events. Was this what real dating was like?—endless hours in torturous, expensive clothing?—humiliating, improbable situations, no doubt conjured up by some puckish higher intelligence? Maybe Carl and I should just spend the rest of our days cruising around in his old man's pickup truck, graduating to picking up widows as we got on in years.

Alice sat up after we dropped off Martha and Carl and started combing her fingers through her disheveled hair, trying to restore some life into the lame curls.

"I'm sorry about tonight," I said. "Everything turned out bad. I couldn't even manage to get you to the Mather Inn."

Alice grimaced. "Oh, I dunno, Buckshot's food wasn't all that bad. At least I'm not hungry anymore." She stopped the finger-combing and turned toward me. "But I've been wondering about one thing. How come you didn't try to get *me* drunk on that spiked punch?"

"You knew about that?"

"You must think girls are pretty dumb. We *all* knew about it."

"Even Martha?"

"Sure. She wanted to see what it was like to take a drink. So . . . why didn't you try to get *me* drunk?"

"I dunno. Didn't think it was a very good idea, I guess. Maybe I was scared of what might happen to you."

Nobody said anything for awhile. Then Alice put her hand on my arm—just a light touch. It was like an electric shock. I was dead tired, but it reenergized me. I shot a quick glance at her and caught her looking at me. I knew we would never skin weasels together again.

In front of her house I turned off the Chevy's engine. Wisps of steam rose from underneath the hood. Patti Page began singing "The Tennessee Waltz" on the Motorola. I quickly reached over to turn it off.

"Leave it on," Alice said.

"I thought you hated that song."

"I really kind of like it. Besides, it seems like years ago since we were dancing to it. And you know something? We didn't get to finish the last waltz."

"What?"

"At the prom . . . Frankie Dominic dropped his accordion on the floor, remember?"

I laughed.

"Want to finish it now?"

"What . . . here? On the street?"

"Why not? No one's awake yet."

We got out of the car. The music drifted faintly from the car window. I put my left hand up in the standard position, but she put both arms around my neck. I had no choice but to put mine around her waist. I felt wonderful. My box step glided effortlessly over the uneven ground. Pre-dawn raindrops began to splat in the dirt, but we didn't care.

One—two—three, *one*—two—three . . .

Biography

Jerry Harju was born in Ishpeming, Michigan, in 1933. He received a degree in engineering from the University of Michigan in 1957 and a MS from the University of Southern California in 1985. After thirty years as a manager in the aerospace industry in Southern California, Jerry began writing as a second career. His first three books, *Northern Reflections, Northern DLights,* and *Northern Passages* are collections of humorous short stories about his experiences growing up in Michigan's Upper Peninsula. His fourth book, *The Class of '57,* takes readers along a humorous and nostalgic path during Harju's

six years, of "higher education" at the University of Michigan. University life then—with its 1950's attitudes on world affairs, morality, and women's roles in society—was vastly different from today. Jerry's fifth book, *Cold Cash*, is a truly wacky novel with an Upper Michigan setting about two down-on-their-luck heroes who plan the perfect bank heist. There are a few complications, not the least of which are two women.

Harju now lives in Marquette, Michigan, spending his time writing books and newspaper columns and travelling all over the globe.